# sparkling. nothing.

Younger Charles Robbins

Published by Adjar, LLC 2022
Younger Robbins: Member Adjar, LLC
Logo design: Erin Cathcart

Cover art by:
Chris Mott
@chrismottart

ISBN: 979-8-218-06216-3

This is a work of fiction.
Any relation to true events is purely
coincidental.

Excerpts of original text appear from
Fyodor Dostoevsky pg. 47 and Henri
Moissan & Victor Lenher pg. 52

Thank You

*Maine, 1933*

The stage was comprised of the same boards as floor, walls, ceiling, and gangway of the old Barn. Worn planks, sixteen feet long, planed and set low, flush as possible across the floor where years past solitary bucks would come to lay and where the buggy teams were washed and brushed and oiled, flapping their gums, gnashing their teeth, glad for relief from the bit and work their proud bodies had done. In a box that would have slept a stable boy if the farm was still working sits a woman who was alive before the Barn was built. From her fingers tinkle the familiar notes of Gershwin, or some other famed composer, while local patrons and tourists file in to be seated on benches and folding wooden chairs.

The weekend-night shows were the most oppressive. When the jungle humidity of the northeast in summer would fill the Barn like a slow cooker. When the smell of booze could be smelled in the dooryard and even in the wings if the players were in particularly good spirits. The one or two spotlights used to light the action onstage would burn, and the show would start, and the cigarettes were lit, and the sweat poured out so you'd have swore it would turn to steam if it wasn't for the puddles under your arms and in your shoes.

It was on those barn boards I had earned my keep all summer, painting and sweeping and assisting in the building of sets: cherry blossom trees and ornate wedding arches. Early on in the summer, it had been *A Midsummer Night's Dream, 1595– William Shakespeare* followed by *The Mikado, 1885–Gilbert and Sullivan* and *The H.M.S. Pinafore, 1878–Gilbert and Sullivan* to finish out the season. The plots in all were perhaps beyond my comprehension but the scenes that played out around me onstage, immersed in the world of Puck's misadventure and poor little Buttercup, I couldn't help but be swept up in the Americanized operatics of great works from before my short lifetime.

The lead players trucked in from New York, Chicago, or even Boston like myself and had performed back and forth on the Broadways of those aforementioned cities. Through Equity arrangements, they would receive room and board and like myself, were indentured to the theatre for the summer months. If I had the inclination I could have most likely followed in the same footsteps as some of the seasoned veterans I had guilelessly befriended, making a name for myself belting out savoy operas and producing one-act plays, sleeping on couches throughout the region, standing in line for Equity checks which were still a state away when I needed them in and out of my pocket several times already, and if I'm lucky, not slicing off my thumb constructing a set of steps on casters to be wheeled around during a musical number.

Though the lives of those folks ten or so years my senior were stockpiled high with anecdotes of late nights and indiscriminate hell-raising, it was hard for me to find much importance in the overall, what-for of it—especially with half the country eating at handout lines and more than half the banks closing their doors on empty vaults.

My old man, whose name was also Joe, had driven up here with me from Western Mass, pleased with the thought of returning to a house with nothing in it but his wife and the absence of a third mouth to feed.

"Settle Down," he had said when the radio broadcast touted the formation of the WPA as an open playing field for socialism. When the radio broadcast fizzled out somewhere in the middle of Maine he extrapolated on the importance of what I was doing for the summer and how Roosevelt himself would be proud because I was taking part in what the New Deal was all about, and how $28 dollars a week plus a commute was enough to support a family of three, but not down-playing the fact that though I was only in my third year of high school—which I should finish—how important it was to learn to earn my keep and also, "don't get too drunk that you throw up and don't knock anyone up."

Those words were long in my history, and I had already experienced a handful of much too drunken nights with the likes of some of the older equity guys—at the homes converted into apartment buildings where they lodged—on swill bought with their summertime retainer and on the credit I was worth each week paid to me in cash by the stage managers at the Barn.

As for the other, I had come close but was none too invested in the options beyond the youngest one of three little maids: my age, unencumbered by want or knowledge of the struggling working class, the daughter of a commercial—including the Barn—landowner. Samantha, who I would watch during rehearsal, performing the semi-native Japanese choreography taught to the maids by a dance instructor from somewhere outside of Chicago. Except for her resentment of the smell of alcohol, the company I kept, the way I walked, and how I appeared, I could tell I was Samantha's type and didn't mind making it known. She had an older sister, Betsie, who was close with Richie, one of my better acquaintances and renter of a couch I would regularly sleep on at a house on Ocean Street in lieu of sacrificing a portion of my pay back to the Barn for lodging. It was through Richie that I received most of my advice on women and life and purpose that summer, and if there was anyone more smart or better educated, I hadn't met them and I didn't care to.

Richie learned philosophy and art in Chicago and started hanging around the theatre scene working ensemble during the weekends and bar backing at clubs on off days. He smoked reefer, he played cards, and more importantly, he put in kind words about me to Samantha's older sister, which at this time was about the best thing I could hope for and a very lousy shot at that.

Late on a Wednesday after rehearsal, Richie had taken Betsie and me up to Old Orchard Beach for a few drinks and to get out of the sticks, which is what Richie called the small town of Ogunquit where we lived these months. Samantha didn't take much to going to the pier or the club and most likely wouldn't have been caught dead four people tight in a three-seat truck with marijuana smoke pouring out the windows.

There was a show onstage—some crooner—and I sat at the bar. Richie had taken Betsie up front to be starry-eyed and smiling. One of those smirky smiles women give you that make you want to need to repent. Betsie was a looker after all, and always seemed to be turned-out everywhere she went in a fancy dress with the diamonds Richie had saved for in her ears. Long, brown—maybe red—hair, sometimes worn up, or sometimes blowing all around like she was on a beach some-where in a movie. She wore makeup, but you could hardly tell, and by the end of the summer, she tanned so that there wasn't a single place to be found on her body that wasn't sun-kissed.

After the crooner, was dancing, which I wasn't very keen on and got enough of during the choruses in the Barn. I ordered a third beer, slipping a couple nickels out from among the cash in my front pocket and let the bartender keep the change, flipping it into a jar beside him. A guy sidled up next to me at the bar and took a seat at the closest stool disregarding the several other options much less intrusive to my personal space. He had on a suit and tie, not like a working stiff, but he was no pretty boy either, and his face showed where it had been broken and reset.

"Whiskey," he said and drank when it was brought. "Your buddy's quite a dancer." He was talking to me.

"I suppose."

"Not a lot of guys your age in the lounge tonight. You his little brother?"

"What's it to you?"

"Easy," he told me. "I'm only asking you a couple questions."

"I didn't come here to answer questions, mister."

"Sounds good. I'll finish my drink and scram."

"That's just fine."

He did like he said and got up to go. He paid with a dollar bill and took the change. Before he left, he slid a paper card up to my half-empty glass. The words were few and easy to read.

Det. James Wallace
FBI

I flipped the card around on the bar.

He watched to see if the gesture had made its effect.

"Tell Richie I was asking about him."

"There's no phone number."

"I'll be around."

The guy left. I pocketed the card and finished my beer before risking a look around the crowded room. The music was too loud for anyone to have heard the conversation. If they had, who cares. No one was looking at me in any particular way. Wallace was nowhere to be seen. The bartender came back around and picked up my empty glass.

"You got smokes," I asked.

He did and offered me a selection.

"Pack of Pall Malls. And another beer and a whiskey."

He gave me a look, but I pulled out the roll of dough I kept stuffed down below the coin money in my pocket and paid with a buck like Wallace before me. That was good enough for the bartender, and he did as he was told, setting me up and sliding an ashtray in my general direction. I tipped a dime, and the bartender poured me another shot.

"On the house," he said, and I liked how it sounded.

I could see Richie dancing up a storm with Betsie down on the floor. They were one of many couples, and sometimes I lost sight of them in the crowd. I folded Wallace's business card and put it with my cash.

*a thing of shreds and patches.*

I rode in the bed of the truck on the way back to Ogunquit. The humidity hung around, trapping the heat of summer. Richie and Betsie had danced for another couple hours, taking breaks to get drinks and pat me on the shoulder. Betsie leaning in with her arms wrapped around Richie's waist.

Whiskey eyes. Perfume sweat. Shining cigarette lips, "Lot of girls out tonight, you don't gotta sit here alone, Joe."

I looked around, "Not really my type."

"Not like what, my sister?" She laughed. Took a hand and put it on my chest. Leaned against me so I had to turn on the stool to stop her from falling. Close enough to feel her whisper, "Not all sisters are the same, Joe."

Now they sat side by side in the three-seater truck with Richie handling the gearshift in between Betsie's knees and punching it on the straightaways so that even over the rush of the warm gusts of nighttime wind, I could hear her squealing and knew that she was batting Richie away with one hand

and pulling him closer with the other. I laid with my hands clasped, keeping my head from bouncing on the corrugated bed, but in my mind I was fingering Wallace's business card, folding it and unfolding it again, wishing for a way to verify the information on it, imagining that I would find Wallace and throw it in his face and tell him to stay away from my friends and me. I thought about taking it out right now and throwing it over the side of the truck. Let the wind take it to the sea, where it would never bother me again.

*

Morning on the couch. Awake before everyone in the three-story colonial which housed Richie and several other guys on the upper floors who would soon all wake and shake off their various nights-before. Betsie would leave Richie alone in his room, rushing to get home before her father got up and was capable of seeing through his own last night. That's when I would walk the two miles back from the small-town streets of Ogunquit and into the farmlands, which lined the eventually unpaved roads. It was my task to open up the Barn in the early mornings and to air out the dressing rooms. I'd brew coffee in the back stage kitchen and drink a couple of full mugs before making more for the others. There were chickens in the yard who's eggs needed to be taken and who's pens needed to be shoveled. The fresh eggs, I'd leave on the back porch of the farmhouse—home to the manager of the farm and Barn alike. The chicken shit went in a compost heap, black gold to be thrown on the vegetable garden in the fall.

Soon, regularly hired men would arrive to harvest the back acre hay fields. They would come through the summer over the rolling White Mountains and reap each field as it was ready before returning to their respective towns and homes in preparation for winter. The fields were bare now with tall piles of hay in bales laid out every hundred feet or so, evidence of the work done that summer.

"These fields have been harvested for hundreds of years," one of the hired farmers told me, "could be, the same roots that some Algonquian chewed on before it was taken from him, could be that's the same stuff I've been kicking around in all these summers. I'll be buried in it before they stop cutting it." He would return when the weather was more mild to carry the cured bales to the Barn before the frost.

Another cast was rehearsing for the show that would run after ours. When they were finished, I would clear and clean the stage of set pieces and trash before wheeling in the many blossomed cherry tree set piece for our evening performance. I spent the rest of the morning pulling nails and breaking down retired props, saving the wood for use on future projects.

Before everyone else arrived for show time, I went to sit in the shade at the back of the shed. I got Wallace's card out of my pocket and looked at it: creased as hell but still the same words. They had been weighing on me all day, and finally, I had come to the conclusion that it was best to tell Richie what had happened and to see how he reacted. Otherwise, I was going to drive myself nuts.

I lit up a smoke from the pack I had bought last night and waited for Richie. He would usually come looking for me back here to bum one or tell me some phony story full of him saving lives and winning big money before losing it all, which was supposed to have happened since whenever I had seen him last, which was never that long.

I had smoked two of the smokes and could hear the cast clamoring into the back stage of the Barn. I trashed the two butts and rubbed my hands in the grass, hoping to conceal the smell of smoke in case I came across Samantha.

She arrived with Betsie, who I tried not to acknowledge too much, hoping that she hadn't mentioned to Samantha how I was out all night in a bar. She was from the same family as her sister—no doubt—but all that had developed and worn on Betsie was still so far off for her younger sister, who possessed the same confidence that made Betsie such a hot ticket but which came out as shrewdness or even judgment and many times was directed clearly at me.

"Hey, Samantha, you look nice."
"You smell like smoke."
"Is that so? Must be from cleaning up butts out here."
"Same as every day."
"What did you do this morning?"
"I had a lesson."
"Anything fun?"
"Hardly."
She began to walk away.

It was a brutal exchange, but worth it to talk to her. If only I could get her to come out at night with me and Richie and Betsie, then maybe she'd loosen up and we could find something to relate on. Everyone's much easier to get along with after a couple of drinks and some reefer.

Pre-show preparations had been made, concessions served, seats filled, and it had come very close to showtime in the old Barn.

Most of the players were standing ready for the overture to begin, cueing the end of reality for the next couple of hours. I had changed from my grimy work clothes into a robe and sandal thing picked out for the ensemble. This is the time that I would usually be looking for Samantha, trying to steal a moment or two with her before the curtains were up.

Tonight was different. I found myself with Betsie waiting in the wings. Richie—the wandering minstrel he—had still not shown up.

"When's the last time you saw him?"

"What are you so worked up for?" Was all she cared.

"It's not like Richie to miss a show is all."

"You were there yourself last night. He was pretty tight, he's probably sleeping it off."

"Right... shouldn't someone go and try to get him?"

"You gonna run the two miles there and carry his drunken ass back? Relax, Joe."

"What about the show?"

"Danny knows the part. He's already in costume."

She was right. It was probably nothing... but she didn't have some FBI man's card burning a hole in her pocket.

All I could think of until the show was over and I had swept the dust from the stage on the last of the straggling audience was about going and showing Richie the card and finding out what he was into.

I changed from my costume as soon as I could and didn't even look for Samantha before running the two miles to the Ogunquit neighborhood. The house was still empty. Front door locked. I found the extra key hidden under a brick over the doorframe and used it to unlock the door. I put the key back in its hidey-hole and went inside.

The whole place was dark. If Richie was still here, he was sleeping one off as Betsie had guessed. I switched the lights on in the kitchen before going into the living room, pushing back the dark as I went, feeling very alone, and wondering if any of the other actors or tourists on the block would be around at this time on a weekend. I thought that I might be the only one in the whole neighborhood, all of Ogunquit for that matter, the entire world. Maybe Richie had only disappeared because I had left this morning. Now that I had left the Barn, the others would be gone too, and if I tried to return home, my mother and father would be gone as well.

Richie hadn't disappeared. I could see his form sprawled out on the bed like Betsie had guessed.

"Hey, Richie. You really blew it today, pal." I turned on the light and approached him. I even shook him by the arm before noticing I was standing in a pool of blood spreading out from the mattress and onto the ground. Through the thick mat of Richie's black hair I could see pieces of skin torn back, exposing sheer white bone and a slushy pinkish-grey mess that I could not clearly distinguish before turning away and vomiting all over the floor.

Richie had been dead since the early afternoon. By the time everyone had filed into the Barn when I was smoking my second smoke earlier in the night, he was already gone. The entire town must have turned out when the police showed up with their flashing lights. Whoever was leftover showed up to see the coroner wheeling six feet of nothing into the back of a station wagon. I was standing outside a ring of people who had formed, smoking one of the few smokes I had left. Betsie was in hysterics nearby, bawling into Danny's shoulder. A collection of most of the theatre people had formed around them. I wasn't really in the mood and was having a hard enough time keeping the image of Richie's brains out of my head without talking about it. I had already suffered the telling once to a couple of cops and then again to a sergeant and again to the captain who had finally arrived, each wanting to know more out of pure disbelief than for any matters pertaining to a case. They had left me alone after that, asking me to please stick around long enough to answer any other questions they might have.

I stuck around, smoking and considering what a person would have to do to deserve what Richie had got done to him, then considered what it was exactly that Richie could be capable of doing, and wondered, had I said anything—had I shown him the business card—something would have happened different. He could have had a chance.

Surrounding faces took on the look of one. Expressions molded in unison, obscured in the nicotine haze. It took me a while to focus and realize what I was looking at. Standing next to the police captain looking in my direction, motioning to where I stood. Wallace.

I killed the cigarette in my hand and walked away through the throng of bystanders, all stupefied and taking mental notes for the grand retelling of the evening's events, which they were lucky enough to see. Wallace was pushing his way in my direction. I ducked into a side yard, cutting an angle from town to the Barn, avoiding the roads altogether, doing my best to break away, and didn't stop running until I had cleared the back acres leading up to the Barn.

I hopped the fence at the yard and went to the familiar area behind the shed where I could sit and catch my breath and dry my face, wet with tears from the brisk air and from something else too. I smoked until my hands stopped shaking and, when I could stand, walked around the side of the shed but hung back before passing the corner. I could see, though only faintly, the outline of a person poking around the back of the Barn. My heart reinstated itself in my throat—a position it had become accustomed to the last few hours. The person was looking for something. It couldn't be Wallace, he was much larger than this guy. He could have sent someone to snoop around. Maybe Richie wasn't who the feds were after. At first, I had thought Wallace might have tracked him here because of an old drug peddling rap, or something like that. But with Richie dead, my mind was spinning, and the possibilities were endless. For all I knew, I had spent the summer drinking booze and getting stoned with a political revolutionary, or even a communist. And for all I knew, this was the guy he was working with or the guy who killed him. He kept nosing around and eventually found the back door to the Barn. He hadn't opened the door half a foot when I found myself approaching, striding brazenly across the yard.

"Stop right there, mister." It was me talking. I didn't even know why I was walking over there, and now I was talking.

The guy froze, and so did I. "I have a gun," I lied, "a pistol. Don't even move." He didn't. "Are you looking for Richie? Are you the guy that shot him?"

I felt very odd standing there unarmed making threats—not getting answers—and when the guy started to approach, it didn't occur to me to remind him of the pistol or even run away. I had run quite a bit already, and if that was all the night had in store for me, then to hell with it, I'll take the dawn standing still.

"Joe? Is that you?" It was Samantha.

"What are you doing here?"

"I'm looking for an earring, I dropped it here I think, Daddy gave them to me, and I was wearing them in my costume."

I lit a match. We both crouched near the wall of the Barn, looking for any glint of the stone. Samantha's eyes found my face in the wavering glow. Her expression changed.

"Have you been crying?"

"Mostly 'cause I was running." The match went out.

"Did you say someone shot Richie?"

"Yeah," I told her.

"How do you know?"

"I'm the one who found him."

In the darkness, I felt her on me, her arms around me, could smell her hair like wildflowers.

"My God, you poor thing. But wait, what about Betsie?"

"She knows."

She stood, before I could even think to put my hands out and around her.

"Where is she?"

"Last I saw she was being taken to the police station."

"I have to go see her. You'll be okay?"

"Yeah, I'll stay here."

"Okay. I'm sorry Joe, I know you and Richie were friends."

"Go take care of your sister."

She left. I leaned on the wall of the Barn and lit up another smoke. I tossed the match in the dewy grass, sizzling before it smoldered out, glinting off a diamond which lay embedded in the ground. I bent to pick up the earring, which was heftier than I imagined, not cheapie stuff, could even be real. Her family could afford it, I suppose. I pulled some of the tobacco out from a fresh smoke and pressed the earring into the paper, covering it back up with the excess leaf. I'd give it back to Samantha next time I saw her as long as I remembered not to accidentally smoke it in the meantime.

Judging by the moon, it was already very late. Too late to sneak into the boarding house where I stayed when I wasn't sleeping on Richie's couch. I considered the cot I had made for myself to nap in the shed, then wandered away from the yard and out to the street.

The unceasing country noises tried their best to keep me distracted, but it wasn't long until I realized where I was headed. I made it to paved road and then sidewalks and was on Richie's porch retrieving the secret key. The crowd had dispersed. The police had taped off the front door. I kind of untaped it and then put it back the best I could. The place was empty. The rest of the guys were all crashing somewhere else. I did what I usually did and went right into Richie's room.

His body wasn't there. That was about the only difference between now and the last time I had come. There was still a sort of outline in the mattress and blankets where a person would have slept. The blood was starting to dry up. You could hardly tell where I had tossed my lunch. It was odd standing there in the moonlit room with the memories of the previous tenant. Now it was someone else's problem, a dirty room, a dip in income for the landlord.

For all of his personality, Richie had lived a simple life, reflected in the state of my surroundings. The only furniture in the whole room—large enough to be a parlor for several guests—was a bed and an old milk crate that served as night stand, dinner table, extra seating. There was no lamp except the ceiling fixture controlled by a push-button switch near the entrance. Many nights I knew Richie would lay in the dark, smoking, reading by penlight, not bothering to get up and hit the switch, knowing he would only have to do so again before falling asleep. I didn't bother with the switch now either, actually spotted the penlight on the milk crate. I picked it up and examined the silver shaft, twisting it. The light turned on. I turned it off, then on again. There wasn't much else on the table: Richie's switchblade, the craggy wooden handle smoothed from his grip. The blade flipped out. It was small but kept sharp. I flipped the blade closed and slid the knife into my back pocket. He had a few bucks in his billfold, which I unceremoniously pocketed—I didn't feel great about doing it, but I also knew it's what Richie would have done if he were here instead. There was an I.D. card in there too: Ricardo Di Giulio, with all the other pertinent information. There was also half a pack of smokes, which I took, adding them to my own stash.

I passed the light over the ground near the bed, forcing myself to look at the blood again. The pool had filled quickly, amassing in what must be a dip in the floor from some sinking joist in the basement. The pool was almost a perfect circle except for where I might have stepped in it earlier and right up under the bed near the wall where there was a smear about as wide as one of the planks in the floor.

The blood didn't seem to have been disturbed, more like it had been drawn over there, finding a crack in the base-board and siphoning itself down into a gap in the wall. The penlight revealed a gap in the boards right under the bed-post. I crouched, leaning over the puddle. Held the light in my teeth and got the switchblade out. Prodded at the board. It didn't move. I levered the knife into the gap. A section of wood no longer than my forearm popped out of place. I shone the light down underneath the floor, revealing a small dugout that Richie must have used as a secret spot. There was a pouch about the size of a baseball down there and from the open neck glittered to life what must have been two or three handfuls of diamonds. They were the size and shape of the one in Samantha's earring but with no backing. A pile of loose stones. I wasn't as cock-sure about pilfering diamonds as I was Richie's spending money, but before I knew it, I had loosened the tie on the pouch and plucked out one of the gems. I pulled out a smoke and stashed the diamond in the filter, tucking it away right next to Samantha's in my pack. I replaced the plank and made it into the living room before turning around and removing the floorboard again. I picked up the pouch, feeling the weight of it in my hand, and stuffed the whole thing in my back pocket.

*a knife in the dark.*

The next few days passed, marked only by the opening and closing of the stage curtain.

Richie's part had been filled by Danny, who knew it well, and I was tasked with filling Danny's role, which had several speaking lines—the first I was ever given. I slept in the shed behind the Barn, and on exceptionally hot nights would lie on the bench outside and count the stars, smoking cigs bought with Richie's spare change.

"Samantha's in a great deal of trouble. She's not allowed to see anyone or leave the house," Betsie had told me.

I pretended not to know why and evaded the subject of any diamond earrings. She didn't talk all that much and seemed pretty dazed. I could have given the earring to Betsie to give to her sister, but I desperately wanted to get the credit for finding it and could only dream of what the reward may be.

When I heard the local cops had called my folks, I imagined I'd get in a little hot water, but supposedly, my old man had only asked if I was fine and if I wanted to stay or come home.

When they didn't have an answer for that, he thanked them and hung up. That's what Captain Montgomery told me when he stopped by the Barn yesterday. He said he talked to my old man himself.

"And hey, Burke," he said to me before leaving, "a couple of my guys said they seen you hanging around your buddy's house. That place is closed off, you understand? Whatever it is you're going through… do it somewhere else. That house is a crime scene."

Every night since Richie was killed, I waited for dinner to be served and for the farmhouse to go to sleep, and I'd walk to Richie's place where I'd stand outside across the street, sit on the stoop sometimes. I never went in again after that first night and hadn't really had any desire to.

When I arrived tonight, I noticed right away that a flashlight jittered around in what was Richie's room. It made me think how obvious it must have been when I was poking around earlier in the week. I crept up the front steps with practiced footfalls knowing all of the places that would deceive me to anyone inside. The crime scene tape was cut back, and the door had been forced open. I could hear someone rummaging around Richie's room looking through the drawers, knocking things over. I crossed the main room silently but stopped about halfway. I heard them shuffling around in there, the short squelch of wood being pried. I could see the form doubled over, rooting around up to the elbow in the floor, not finding what was supposed to be there. The intruder stood and came my way. I pulled the knife from my pocket, flipped the blade, considered the chance of making it to the front door from here without getting shot. The flashlight found me in the center of the room.

"Turn off that light. You can see it from the street."

"Christ, kid, ya scared the ever-lovin' shit outta me."

It was immediately apparent that this guy was not from around here. I wasn't so familiar with the cities outside of Boston, but Richie was from Chicago, and this guy sounded a lot like him. His gruff voice had a gentle airiness to it. I could make out that he was bald on top of his head but had thick curly black hair over his ears and in the back. He was dressed as though he had come from a shift at the docks with a peacoat wrapped around him.

He killed the light and put it away.

Our eyes readjusted to the moon.

"Who the hell are you," I asked.

"Is that a knife?"

I regarded the blade in my hand, pictured swinging it at the man: his ropey fingers stopping my arm, shaking the knife loose. Another hand around my throat, larynx restricted, capillaries bulging. I switched the blade closed and slid it into my pocket. We stood in the dark, empty-handed.

"You a friend of Richie's or something?"

"I was."

"Geez... look, I can imagine how you feel."

"Did you shoot him?"

"Did I shoot him? Kid, if I shot him, you think I'd be caught poking around here, flapping my gums with you?"

"Then, why are you here?"

"It ain't for the sea air."

*the only one in town and always open.*

We rode in Richie's uncle's Chrysler Imperial. The bench seat was about long enough for me to lay all the way across, and if there were any potholes in the road, the suspension would never let you know. Richie's uncle's name was Salvatore, but he said I could call him Sal.

"Richie's mother sent me out here to take care of any paperwork, collect his things," he told me. "I think she doesn't like the idea of the cops draggin' out girly magazines or whatever it is you guys keep stashed nowadays. Anything like that you think I should know about?"

"Some grass? But we smoked it all the last night I saw him."

We were quiet after that, both picturing the hole in the floor by Richie's bed.

Before we passed entirely out of town, Sal noticed the sign at The Ogunquit Diner.

"You hungry, kid? My treat." He was already pulling onto the strip of asphalt that made up the parking lot of the diner—a patch of fading tar large enough to keep your vehicle off the main drag so long as the tailgate was up.

We got out and went inside together. I had never actually been to the diner and was surprised to see how clean it was. The booths and counters were all modern polished, and the woman behind the counter wasn't some dried up hick but a girl not much older than me. The owner's daughter she told us when we asked.

"Dad left for the night, but I can make the whole menu. What'll ya have?" She proffered a single menu between us.

"Steak," said Sal, "and hash if you got it or any kind of potato." She looked at me.

"Coffee." My gut hadn't completely untwisted since first meeting Sal.

"Cream and sugar?"

"Plenty," I said.

She went to get the coffee, and when she came back looked me over more intently than before.

"Don't I know you?" She poured.

"Not sure."

"You from around here?"

"Staying the summer."

"That's what it is! You work at the Barn." She leaned on the counter with her elbows. "I've seen you up there singing your brains out."

"I mostly build the sets."

"Hmm," she said without parting her lips, which I noticed were a pleasing and natural shade of pink, same as was in her cheeks standing out against her unmarked skin, nourished by the humid sea air. "You know Sam then too? She said you were pretty cute once you took off the face paint and kimono."

"Did she?" My face turned as red as the vinyl cushioned stool.

"No. But you are." She straightened up. "Steak and hash coming up, boys." To Sal, "You're the only one eating?"

"Eat something, kid. My treat." Sal broke in, anxious to see his meal start cooking.

"I'll have the same as him," I told the girl.

She headed into the back part of the kitchen and Sal nudged me in the ribs with one of his meaty elbows. I focused on my coffee, only glancing up to watch the girl through the separation in the kitchen wall where she worked over the grill.

"You hung around Richie's place a lot since..." Sal looked straight ahead.

"Not a lot."

"Nights?"

"Anytime, really."

"You ain't got no one else to hang around with?"

I didn't say yes or no.

"You and him must have had other buddies."

"There's Richie's girl, Betsie."

"You ain't got a girl?"

I looked behind the counter, "Nah."

I drank some more of the coffee. Sal lit up a smoke, which he didn't have time to finish before the food came. We ate, making short work of the meal without any talking. When it was over, I lit a couple more smokes for Sal and me. The girl brought more coffee.

"If you ain't got a place to stay, why not come with me, kid? I got a buddy outside of town. Nice place, plenty of room."

"I don't think so. I gotta' be back at the Barn pretty early."

"You're sure? My buddy, he's got a nice place, good booze too, cask stuff. You look like you could use a good drink and a decent bed."

The girl was wiping down the counter and gave me a look like she agreed with Sal.

"Okay," I told him, and we finished our coffee.

"How's about the check, angel?"

"I'm no angel, mister, and it's not my name either, so you better think twice before calling me it."

"Then what should I call you?"

"Victoria Miller. Vicky if it pleases you."

"Alright, Vicky, how's about the check for me and my friend?"

Vicky scribbled on her order pad in pencil, brown eyes—golden, actually—flickering between the two of us. She tore a page and handed it to Sal. He paid and we turned to go.

"Joe," she called, turning me back. "I work until pretty late most nights. You seem like a bit of a night owl yourself, why don't you come and keep me company sometime. How's that sound?"

"Just fine."

*

The house was on the outskirts of a town called Elliot, touching the Piscataqua River, the border of New Hampshire. The driveway was held in by trees at both sides until, climbing a hill, the terrain opened up. Not hay, but green grass fields appeared on my left. On the right, more forest spotted by a couple of cabins. What looked like a forge built into a shed, rusted over and covered in layers of dust. A pole barn with manual threshers and tractors, the cracked leather on the yolks long faded. The road hugged the tree line until the forest receded and then, on my right, more open land. The shorn grass, acres wide, and in the middle of it a house that looked like one they tell you Thomas Jefferson lived in. The driveway ended in a circle that would lead you out right back the way you came. When we got to a place near the front of the house, Sal stopped the car, killing the engine.

"This is the place, kid."

Sal tossed the car keys in the front seat and lead the way up to the front porch. Voices could be heard through a screen door that had been put up over the grand entryway. Sal ushered me in, letting the screen door close with a slap behind us. A man in a tannish suit made for a bear who didn't waste time appearing stood in front of us and nodded to Sal, who smiled in return.

"The boss in?"

The guy didn't say anything. He turned his head slightly and listened. Sleek black hair brushed the shoulders of his suit. The voices from another room floated over us out the screen door.

"Thanks a lot, Awesus, I'll tip ya on the way out." Sal passed by him.

The guy never responded. He watched us go. Followed not far behind as we made our way into a kind of ballroom that was supposed to be real impressive: polished marble floors, columns, wooden side tables with vases standing out in the middle of nowhere. The second floor had a banister all around it, but I couldn't tell how you would get up there from here.

In the room where the voices were coming from—half office, half library—books lined the walls; books were stacked on the floor. There was office stuff and a desk with a rolling chair on one side. The blinds were drawn tight. The lights were turned all the way up. A fire burned in a granite hearth on the wall. Wood smoke and sage did an okay job of masking it, but the air was as thick with dope as the three owners of the voices we had heard from the yard: a man and two women sitting near a roaring fire. Sal went to the desk, laying down his coat and other various personal articles. I stood in the doorway and took a smoke from the pack. Before I could find a match, my buddy Awesus had a lighter in my face. I used it and nodded my thanks. He extinguished the flame with a flourish and went back to being imposing somewhere on the other side of the room.

One of the women poured green alcohol from a green bottle, her friend brought more glasses. The man stood and walked to the fire, stoking it with one of the blackened tools from the hearthstone. Sal joined him, and they spoke so no one could hear. The girl stopped pouring and brought me a glass of the green stuff. She had on a long silk dressing gown that pressed up against her when she walked so that her form was exposed in a way that was even more tempting than if she wore nothing at all— which I could also picture and wouldn't say no to. She handed me one of the drinks: long fingers, painted nails, silver rings. She leaned in, kissing one of my cheeks and then the other.

She moved on, repeating the gesture with Awesus, leaving him with a glass of the green stuff. He raised his glass in my direction and took a big gulp. I sipped the stuff. It was sweet and bitter at the same time, but it went down smooth, and I felt myself loosen straightaway. The girls poured more green booze for Sal and our apparent host who embraced and then drank with each other before retiring to cushy seats.

"Don't worry, kid. Awesus does a swell job guarding the place. You can take a break," Sal told me.

I joined the group, taking tugs off the glass. The girls were talking, sitting close on a couch with no back and only one arm. Sal leaned back and lit up, settling in. The man looked me over, drinking his drink. Legs crossed, slippers hanging loosely off his toes. His hair was done like Clark Gable, and maybe he thought he looked a little like him too, with a black mustache, oiled hair, and a well-practiced wink to match a toothy grin.

"Sal tells me you were a friend of our nephew."

"He's your nephew too?"

The guy looked at Sal and laughed.

"We have many uncles and nephews and distant relations in our... family."

"Okay," I drank.

"I'm sorry to hear you lost your friend. You can imagine how we feel." The girls had quieted down. Awesus swirled his drink. "Gloria, top off young Joseph's glass for us, will you."

Gloria, the same one who had kissed me, brought the bottle over and topped off my glass. She set the bottle on the mantle next to a wooden case with the image of flowering trees carved into the lid. She took out a thick, rolled cigarette with a golden foil mouthpiece and removed my cig from where it was dangling in my face. Using the burning end, she lit up the gold-tipped stick and inhaled deeply. I could feel the cool bands of silver rings on the back of my neck as she drew me in, bluish smoke swirling in her open mouth, eyes narrowed, dreamy. We kissed, our lips wet with booze. She pushed smoke into my lungs, and I could taste the earthy headiness of the dope. She passed the joint around the room and everyone partook until the ceiling was lost in hazy fog and drinks had been refilled several times.

I sat on the chaise lounge—that's what I was told it was called—with Gloria and her friend. Max—the Clark Gable guy—talked a good deal, sometimes getting up and stoking the fire, opening a book and reading a passage while Gloria and her friend nodded along. I caught Sal's eyelids drooping at times, but when it was offered, he took more drink and puffed on a cigar.

"What do you think about that, Joseph?" Max asked me after a dissertation that I had mentally checked out of.

"Pretty good?"

Max smiled, flashing the perfect teeth.

"He thinks it's pretty good. Any other thoughts?"

"A few. But probably best they don't get formulated."

This made Max laugh. He looked down at Sal, laughing, at the girls, at me, over to Awesus. A forced booming staccato.

"What is it that brought you to the seacoast this summer?" He said, regaining his composure.

"I work at the Barn."

"The Barn?"

"The one where they do the plays, I bet." It was the first time I heard Gloria talk. She touched my arm "Is that right? The play barn?" She had an accent, French? Her hand stayed where it was.

"Yeah, the play barn," I said.

"And that's how you knew our boy Richie! Are you a dramatist, Joseph? Or a singer? You could sing for us right now." Max was pouring and drinking, both hands full.

"I mostly take care of the Barn. Build the sets."

"I see. The working class. Salt of the earth."

"I suppose."

"Was it your idea to go work at the Barn?"

"I suppose not."

"Your father's then?"

"Yeah. He said it'd be good to work, something about eating and having clothes on your back."

"That's good advice. What will you do after the summer?"

"I got school."

"No other plans?"

"What is this mister, you writing a book or something? You get sick of reading all these aloud you gotta' start taking notes on your own? Yeah I got a summer job, I go to school, as soon as I can I'm gonna invest in a better hammer and then retire banging nails, I haven't slept well lately, and I already used the shitter today. You got any more questions I suggest you ask them to yourself cause I'm not long for this place if you know what I mean."

I stood, tossing my cigarette butt in the fire, Gloria tried to pull me back but I brushed her hand aside. I turned my back on the whole merry band and started across the room. Awesus approached as I neared the door but didn't bar my way. I brushed past him and left through the ballroom without looking back.

I had walked for a few miles when the headlights cut across the gravel at my feet. Sal's Imperial rolled up with Awesus behind the wheel. He leaned over and popped open the passenger's door. I considered the road ahead of me—about twelve miles back to the Barn—and got in slamming the door. We drove in silence, the only car with anywhere to be tonight.

"How'd you end up working for a guy like that, like Max?"

"To have clothes on my back, food to eat."

I lit up, "That's just fine."

"Those weren't your father's words?"

"Beat it, ya' bother me. My old man sounds more like that. Fresh air, he says, it's good for ya'. I tell him, we live right by the park. But he doesn't listen."

"You don't like it here?"

"Nice as anywhere, I suppose. What about you? Aren't you supposed to be living on some kind of reservation?"

"Beat it, they said."

I didn't ask why.

"No, bother. I got a few nice suits, I got a nice place to live, women when I want them, cash as I please. I've seen Paris, and Germany, and even China."

"And all you gotta do is listen to that guy yap all day?"

"You don't have to like a guy to take his money."

"You don't have to take the money either."

Old Awes' didn't have anything to say after that. I didn't either. We drove the rest of the way back to the Barn how we had started, in silence with the windows down, letting in the warm gusts of passing nighttime. I had him stop on the road away from the farmhouse.

"Turn your lights off when you turn around," I told him. He swung the boat-of-a-car around and didn't turn his lights back on until he was well out of sight.

I was halfway down the dirt driveway when the bright headlights of a car came bearing down on me. It stopped before I had to dive out of the way, wrapped up in swirling dust. Wallace got out.

"Are you goddamn crazy flashing those headlights around in the middle of the night?"

"Take it easy, Burke."

"Kill the engine, you'll wake the whole house."

He leaned in the car and killed it. No one had stirred in the farmhouse. Wallace was close to me when I turned back. I began to walk away from him, lighting up. He put his hand on my shoulder. I shrugged him off. He grabbed me again, and I flung my smoke at his shoes.

"Buzz off, Dick." I was soused.

"Wise up, Burke I'm trying to tell you some straight dope, you're too busy being one."

"I didn't say anything to Richie, alright. I didn't do what you asked, so I got nothing to do with any of this."

"Where were you tonight?"

"Nowhere."

"You weren't at the house on Ocean Street, I looked."

"I was seeing a girl."

"Tell that to Walter Winchell. I'm looking for facts."

"You got 'em."

"What was her name?"

"Gloria."

"A local?"

"Don't think so."

"A friend of yours?"

"She is now."

"You must be a charmer."

"Not really."

"It practically takes a committee to get my wife in the mood. Charm or none. Unless I get her a little something to grease the wheels. A diamond necklace, last time it was earrings." He glared at me. I didn't respond. "I know you think you got a line on this, but you don't. You're not careful you'll end up wearing an overcoat to match your friend's… Chicago style."

"I got an early rehearsal," I said and walked away.

"I'll be around, Burke."

"Lucky me," not sure if he heard.


I watched from inside the shed as Wallace pulled away. When I was sure he was gone, I snuck out across the yard to the back of the Barn and let myself in. The dressing rooms were pitch black, but I knew my way from the back door past rows of vanity mirrors to a concrete slope leading to the eaves of the main theatre where the moon was able to penetrate the high glass above the front dooryard. I could make out the form of the many blossomed cherry tree. I went around to the back of the trunk and tore out a piece of the patchwork plywood it was made of, revealing my own hidey-hole where no one else was sure to look. I tucked the pouch of diamonds inside, hidden neatly away, and resealed the back of the tree before rolling it out and securing it with a wooden jack, saving myself a few minutes of work in the morning, which would hopefully be spent asleep.

*the early worm.*

The sleep I got was worse than none at all. The time I saved myself the night before was lost when I dropped the morning's first pot of coffee before pouring a cup. I cleaned up and made more, drinking a mug of the second brew before it finished. By the time I shoveled, and poached all the eggs in the coops, I was called to help a group of other stagehands maneuvering a retired set piece into the back of a pickup.

Rehearsals were for the last show of the summer, and when the Monarch of the Sea came on board, I passed out right onstage, three-cheersing my ass backward into the eaves.

I was outback the shed lying in the grass when I was revived by Betsie, who sat on the bench looking down at me.

"You passed out," she said. "They figure it's because of Richie and all that. You been drinking or what?"

"Yeah."

"Tequila, I'd say."

"No. Something else, something green."

"Absinthe?"

"I don't know."

"Why don't you take the day off? You look like hell."

She didn't look so hot herself. Baggy eyes, raw nose, hair pulled back, not even her signature stones in her ears.

"I guess I will."

"Why don't you go see Samantha? She's been asking for you."

"Don't pull my leg, Betsie."

"Forget it then, spend the day passed out in the lawn." She got up to leave.

"Isn't she still in trouble?"

"Daddy won't be home for hours. If he even remembers." She turned to go.

"Hey, Betsie. Where's your earrings, the ones Richie gave you?"

"Daddy said not to wear them for a while. He says even if Richie was a no-count heel, I'm still in mourning and should act like it."

I felt almost sober as I walked the back roads to Samantha's house. Focused on my destination and what I would say when I got there. I had fantasies of Samantha, a sheer summer dress, an empty house. But I knew I was dreaming and would more likely be turned away at the door, maybe by her father himself, back early from whatever business he had taken care of. If that was the case, I figured I'd trudge the miles back to the Barn and give up on the whole thing.

Without Richie or Samantha around, there wasn't much to do. Betsie was no real company. My coming days seemed bleak, filled with cigarette smoking and nail pulling. There was only one more show anyhow. The summer was almost over, and pretty soon, I'd be home. The way things were, my old man might let me keep on working instead of finishing school. His brother had plenty of connections in town. I could get a job roofing and work it straight away until I was eighteen. Head down to Tennessee and get a job building dams.

The estate where Samantha's family lived was even more impressive than Max's. The house could be seen from the road, a single building set in the middle of a sprawling acreage. There were no cars to be seen in the carport. No one was working on the landscaping or around at all. The whole place gave off the feeling of being abandoned except for once I was within earshot, and the wind wasn't blowing, music could be heard billowing from an upstairs window. I found the bell on the front porch and was about to ring it when another sound bounced off the siding, a car coming up the drive behind me. I climbed off the side of the porch and pressed my back up against the corner of the house. This wasn't Samantha's father coming home unannounced. The car rolling up was another I recognized, Sal's Imperial. He pulled up and got out, tossing the car keys in the open window before climbing the front porch steps. I could see the front door if I wanted to stick my neck out but stayed where I was, listening instead. Sal rang the bell, which sounded through the open windows. The phonograph was stopped. Footsteps on stairs. Samantha opened the door, standing inside the threshold.

"How you doin' darling?" Sal addressed her.

"Can I help you?" Her curt demeanor carried through to even this imposing adult.

"Uh yeah. I'm trying to find Mr. Hamilton."

"He's not here."

"Do you know when he'll be back?"

"No. Is that all?"

"You ain't gonna ask me in for a cuppa' water or something?"

"Do you want water? I can bring you a glass."

"No. That's okay. I'll be going now. It was nice to meet you…"
She shut the door. Rough.

Footsteps on stairs again. Presently the music resumed. When Sal had drove out of sight, I cut an angle across the yard back toward the road. I couldn't talk to Samantha now. What are the chances she was ever even asking about me? Slim to none. I got back into the main town of Ogunquit and called a hack. I smoked while I waited for the driver.

"Where to?"

I told him where.

"That's a bit of a haul. You sure you got the dough?"

I did, and we were off. When I offered a smoke, The Hack took it and lit it himself. When he offered me a drink, I took it—and another—before handing the bottle back.

It wasn't until we got much closer the guy ever talked again. He was from around here. Grew up here. Been driving since back before he can remember… which admittedly wasn't that long.

"It used to be you'd wait by the pier. You'd wait there all night in the summah,' and usually, you'd get plenty of rides. Kids coming back from a night out, drunks too tight to get home. Nowadays you wait at the station. No use in burning gas to get to the beach, and people hardly go unless it's the weekend or they know the band. You ever go up there?"

"I've been."

"Not really my kind'a place, but I always did like to see folks come out of there nights. Sometimes one by one, then at the end, swarms of them. Who knows where the hell they're all going. I always liked that. Sit and sip and watch them all walking past. Even times no one was getting in for a ride… I'd sit and watch… coming up with the story for each one, where they was going, if they was in love or not… if they was too young to be out, or if they might have church in the morning."

"How would you ever know if you were right?"

He took another drink.

The ride didn't take as long as it had seemed the first time I made it with Sal. We were cruising along the farmhouses, which made up the bank of the Piscataqua. I pointed out the way as we got close to the turn off for Max's, and the driver slowed, came to a halt, and turned to look at me with a steady, curious eye.

"This the place?"

"Sure enough."

"You a friend'a the family or something?"

"You could say that."

"That's my luck. Drive twenty miles and get stiffed."

"What's the matter?"

"No matter."

I pulled out some cash, but the guy wouldn't have it.

"I'm not interested in any free rides, mister."

"Your money's no good here."

"When's that ever been true? Take the dough."

"Look, you want to do me a real favor? Get me a bottle of the good stuff."

"Booze?"

He laughed, "not milk."

"I don't really know if I can–"

He was already throwing the car into gear and reaching his hand out to pass me a company card, type printed on the front, handwritten on the back.

"Give me a call if you need a lift."

The Hack left me standing alone with the card in my hand.

I found the Imperial parked at end of the roundabout driveway. The day had broken and begun to cool. The music of birds calling home to nest overcame the hours-long buzzing of unseen cicadas. I went up the porch, half expecting to see Awesus there waiting for me. He wasn't, so I made my way through the lobby, through the ballroom and into the study. All empty. I poked around. Nothing had changed except the ice in the buckets. Betsie was right, the label on a green bottle said it was Absinthe—whatever the hell that was—and I could do without any for a long time coming. I checked the cabinets for a real drink and found several unmarked bottles filled with shades of brown liquor. I popped the cork on one and took a pull: rye. Thanks, Max.

I plopped into the big armchair designated for the man himself and put my feet up on his hassock. The rye was quality, much better than The Hack's, with none of that isopropyl taste cheapie stuff gets. I picked up the book that was open nearest to me and flipped a couple pages. The whole thing was in some other language with flowery illustrations on the sides. In another nearby book, I found the translation. It appeared that Max was in the process of converting the entire text by hand. I flipped through his version, reading here and there...

Sometimes you dream strange dreams, impossible and unnatural; you wake up and remember them clearly, and are surprised at a strange fact: you remember first of all that reason did not abandon you during the whole course of your dream; you even remember that you acted extremely cleverly and logically for that whole long, long time when you were surrounded by murderers, when they were being clever with you, concealed their intentions, treated you in a friendly way, though they already had their weapons ready and were only waiting for some sort of sign; you remember how cleverly you finally deceived them, hid from them; then you realize that they know your whole deception by heart and merely do not show you that they know where you are hiding; but you are clever and deceive them again—all that you remember clearly.

For all I knew, he was making it up as he went along. I had almost finished my second glass of rye when I heard the sound of laughter somewhere outside. I put the books how I thought I'd found them and went to the nearest window. The shades had still not been pulled. I drew one aside. Out back of the house was another yard, same as the front: sprawling, green. A patio had been built under the shade of some oak trees with flagstones. Gloria was out there with her friend lying in a lounger together like the cover of some magazines

I had seen. The peaks and valleys of their landscape visible as though the material they wore was only a pleasing glow.

I took the rye out to the back yard holding the bottle in the crook of my arm while I lit up. When I got closer, I could see that Gloria was reading while her friend rested her head on her chest with her eyes closed. She was the opposite of Gloria in appearance with the shiny blonde hair of a movie star and bright eyes to match. If she ever opened her mouth to talk, I would imagine she be from Texas or California. She didn't talk, and Gloria stopped reading.

"Hey there, Gloria."

"Hello, Joe. It's nice to see you again today. I hope you weren't too upset last night."

"Not too. Is Sal around?"

"I'm not sure. I've been here in the yard with Rochelle all day. It was too beautiful to go inside."

"I've been outdoors all day too. Listen, if Sal comes around, will you tell him I was looking for him?"

"If I see him."

"What about Max? You seen him today?"

"Max is never much fun before evening. I've been outside here all day. Isn't it beautiful?"

"I better let you get back to it. Tell those guys I was looking for them."

"You didn't bring any glasses for that bottle?"

"I suppose not."

"That's okay. We all can share."

She held out her hand for the bottle, drinking a couple of times before asking her friend, "Boire un verre?"

Rochelle sat up and took the bottle, leaning into her friend, resting the glass on her lower lip, tilting gently.

"Why don't you sit with us? We would like the company."

Gloria scooted over and motioned for me to sit with them on the lounger. It was almost dusk. The whole yard had that not real feeling that comes with the close of a summer day. The bottle made a revolution between us, then another. Our touches lingered, no longer drinking. The bottle went away. I felt the cool silver of Gloria's rings on my neck again. She pressed my palm to her breast. Rochelle overlapped my hand with hers, pressed her body against mine. Gloria drew me closer, turning away so that my mouth was against her neck. Black hair brushing over my eyes. I kissed her neck. She dug her nails into my jeans. I bit down above her earring and she laughed. I kissed her face and found that her lips had already met Rochelle's. My hand slipped below a dress and found skin, like a steel brush on porcelain, but Rochelle didn't mind. She squeezed her legs together, trapping me there. Soon she had her friend tilted back with her dress hiked up to her belly. I watched as Rochelle kissed and licked at the insides of Gloria's thighs. Gloria clutching onto blonde hair, taking short breaths, her teeth working her bottom lip.

I eased myself back out from under my new pals and stood. It was an honor to be involved, but it seemed I wasn't needed. I went for the whiskey and Gloria grabbed onto my arm.

I stepped closer. She began to unclasp my belt.

The moon came, making paler our naked bodies in its glow.

I woke up on the lounger with Rochelle asleep on my arm. We had been covered by a blanket. Gloria was gone. I found my pants and worked a smoke out from the pocket with my free hand. I folded a match back on its packet and snapped my fingers. The sulfur peaked and idled.

Rochelle didn't stir until the smoke was almost done. She took it from me and finished the rest of the stick while I got dressed. I found the rye where I had left it and took a drink. I offered Rochelle, but she shook her head, no.

It had got late fast. The whole estate was dark except for where cracks in Max's heavy curtains revealed some life inside the house. Rochelle took my hand in hers. We walked the long way around the back of the grounds, holding hands, listening to the noise of the unseen river.

"Will you stay here with me for the night?" She spoke slowly, working her way through the accent.

"It looks like I already am."

"Max will not mind. If you're thinking that."

"I'm not."

We walked like that for a while longer, ranging the entire property finding the water, and then the tree line. Every now and then, some small animal would skitter away, cracking the underbrush as we approached, and Rochelle would call it as though she had seen it.

"A fox," she said.

Her father's family were trappers, then loggers.

"Goddamn the Queen," he had said, and then came to work the mills around Auburn and Lewiston.

"My father told me I was born on the munitions plant floor and that my mother went back to work the very same day."

"Tough chick."

"How can I know if it's true? He was fighting the Germans in Champagne. He didn't see her again because she died in the factory, on the same floor where I was born. From TNT."

"An explosion?"

"Poison. Her hands were still yellow when they buried her. I was only a little girl then, but I remember."

"Where's your father now?"

"Dead. And yours?"

"Massachusetts."

We crept back inside after everyone had gone to sleep.

Rochelle lead the way upstairs. The bedroom was small but real fancy. Polished wood floors and four a poster bed. She undressed, and so did I, holding each other close. I kissed her and she didn't let me stop. We found the bed, never parting. As the moon had come before, so did the sun, though we couldn't tell through the tightly shut blinds.

The little clock on top of last year's Farmer's Almanac at the bedside told me the outside world had already neared midday. Rochelle had stayed nuzzled against me all morning. I got a smoke from my pack next to a vial of pills by the Almanac. There was another book with several scraps of paper sticking out as place holders.

\*

*"The Electric Furnace" by Henri Moissan & Victor Lenher:*
Experiments Under Pressure

The highest temperatures commonly attained in the arcs are between 1700° and 1800°. In our laboratory furnaces we do not often attain, even with gas carbon, above 1500° to 1600°. Under these conditions, certain experiments become difficult to conduct, and scientific investigations find their limits in the fusion points of refractory clay and porcelain... the solution of the problem is theoretically very simple. It consists in placing in the smallest possible cavity, some distance above the substance to be heated, an arc of great intensity. The difficulties appear only when we attempt to incorporate these ideas into an easily handled and inexpensive form of apparatus. The forms of apparatus which I describe in this chapter are the first in which the action of the heat of the current may be clearly separated from electrolytic action. Previous to our researches, various attempts had been made to use the high heat furnished by the electric arc.

One of the transparent diamonds (Fig. 32) measured 0.38 mm. or about 0.4 mm. in its longest direction. Its appearance was characteristic; it sank in methylene iodide, and disappeared by burning in the small platinum boat at 900° with the formation of carbon dioxide. On carefully withdrawing the boat from the tube in which the combustion was made, in the place of the small fragment, there was found a trace of ash, scarcely visible under the microscope, which preserved the original shape and which had a yellow-gray color...

A beautiful, clear and well-crystallized diamond...

I finished the smoke and left the book where I'd found it. Rochelle didn't wake up when I went to her washroom to clean up or when I pulled my clothes on and sneaked out. The downstairs was still empty. The whole house must be on the same schedule. I found the kitchen—an old servant's style type with double-stacked ovens and a big sink basin. There was a double stovetop boiler for coffee, and I used it. In the back of the kitchen was a swinging door—about a third the size of average. I pushed it open with my toe and could see into a stairwell of equal proportions.

The narrow stairway was carpeted, worn thin in the center where a blackened trail was walked after years of use. The banister—filled with nicks and scrapes—lead up to a landing that branched off in three directions to the second floor. Another corridor lead down toward what was presumably the basement. There were no stairs, only a gradual incline. The walls in the slanted hallway were different than any I had seen in the house: first the normal wood paneling, then some average plywood stuff, then granite rocks, which jutted out at odd angles held together by hundred-year-old masonry, and then neatly laid brick with new grout.

Our root cellar back home was usually about twenty degrees cooler than the hottest point of any day. Ma keeps potatoes and onions down there because of it. This place was warm, balmy. The ramp leveled out and opened up, the bricks forming an arch overhead. At the end, I was faced with a door fit for a tool shed. Untreated wood planks made up the wall and in the center a door with a latch and no handle. I flipped the latch and opened the door.

The basement room I entered was nothing like the one where Ma kept the onions. The roof expanded over my head. The air was moist with steam and smelled of hot grain.

Polished steel silos affixed to the back wall, each one with shining limbs reaching out across the floor, some ending at barrels where a recognizable liquid dropped slowly, languidly filling the wooden casks. Other extremity pipes reached up to the ceiling and out of view, carrying exhaust back out to the above-ground world. Pallets full of the barrels were stacked around the concrete floor like bales of hay, all branded with dates on the side. Some going back as many as ten years. Next to the casks were other crates with chalk markings: (CaO), (Fe), (Pt). Across the floor was a set of steps with more casks; crates full of sealed bottles piled around. Built next to the steps was a sort of elevator platform operated by chain pulleys. Above the platform, there was a double basement door that swung out. I used the steps and pushed one side open then climbed out. I found myself on the bank of the river standing next to a concrete ramp leading down to the water. Parked at the end of the ramp, lashed down and bobbing slightly in the wake of the river was a raft boat on pontoons.

"We're having breakfast in the house." Awesus was standing behind the basement entrance.

We walked back over the grounds together toward the house. There was no sign of the underground bunker where I had been.

Old Awes' wasn't lying. Breakfast was on with biscuits, and ham, and eggs, and fruit, and more coffee, and fresh juice.

"Good morning, Joseph! I see you've allowed us to welcome you into the fold."

"Yeah. How's it going?"

"It goes. Isn't that what they say?"

"Sure."

"Have a seat. Have some more coffee. And juice! Are you starved? You must be. I am." He kissed Gloria's hand, who was seated next to him at the room-length breakfast table.

I sat a few chairs away, giving them space. Rochelle came in and sat next to me, Awesus across from us.

"Where's Sal?" I asked.

"He had to go into town. Something about funeral arrangements. Dreadful." He began to pile food onto a dish as he spoke, placing the plate in front of me. He went on, in turn, making heaping offerings to the others. The food was good. The coffee he poured was much better than the stuff I made, and we all sat together, a big screwy family.

Rochelle ate quietly and barely anything at all. Max and Gloria spoke together between bites. Awesus was finished first and smoking. He offered me the same, and I joined him. Max himself cleared the table, leaving behind our coffees and the pot. He lit a pipe when he returned, and Gloria topped off his cup. Max ran his thumbprint along the edge of the china, examining the design painted on the porcelain as if they weren't his cups that he'd drank out of a hundred times before, not looking up as he spoke,

"You've had some time to explore the grounds. Do you like what we have to offer?"

Pretty solid set up you got going. No wonder your rye has been so nice to me."

"And Rochelle? She's pleasant company, isn't she? I think the girls were getting bored here with only me."

"No, Max," Gloria broke in. "We love it here."

He patted her bare knee.

"Yes, I know we all have fun. But we need change! You see Joseph, we're all using you in a way to stave off the melancholia of a prosperous life lived… not too well."

"Glad I could help."

"Glad! What a remarkable way to put it. Aren't we all glad?" The heads at the table nodded. "And even more so now, do you know why," no one had time to answer, "because we get to take our new guest out on the town and show him off. Doesn't that sound like a ball, Joseph?"

"I'm still not exactly sure what it is."

"A party, what else could we need? We've been cooped up here too long! Our bouquets have dried, and garland rotted, leaving only the spirited remembrance of that happier time, the past."

*dead man's party.*

I spent the evening reading through some of Max's many volumes and helping myself to his variations on brown liquor. Sal didn't come back that day. I didn't ask about him again. Rochelle and Gloria remained hospitable, but a vagueness had come over them both that was unlike the daytime stupor of booze or even good grass.

Now that it was dark and they had a few drinks in them and we were out speeding down back roads in Max's Roadster, him driving like a madman—keeping one hand on a bottle of champagne and another on Gloria—the girls were in high spirits again, squealing and laughing, sitting up high on the backs of the seats.

I sat squeezed up against Awesus, who smoked complacently on a funny stick, which I took gratefully when offered.

We left the town of Elliot by some back road and it wasn't long before I could recognize where I was. I had walked this same road yesterday back and forth, and now as the miles burned under us, I was sure that we were heading to the very same end.

There were only so many properties around here, and the chances slimmer than none that Mr. and Mrs. Mullaghanee, the cheese farmers, were hosting any type of haute affair.

Max eventually slowed down long enough for me to unclench, and I hit the reefer one last time trying to settle my gut. I hadn't handled the ride as well as my stony-faced friend who hadn't even removed his white Stetson the entire time. The only piece of Awesus that seemed at all disturbed was the strap of his bolo tie. He flipped the feathered end off his shoulder where it had blown and adjusted his collar in the front.

The whole lot of us looked pretty good: Awesus in his white suit, Max in an all-out monkey suit, and me in one to match.

"Borrow one from my son," he had said, "he won't miss it."

The girls were all diamonds and pearls with bands in their hair and holders for their cigs. I didn't have to try hard to hear the music coming from the windows this time. The Hamilton's place was all lit up like Gatsby's, with bare bulbs strung tree-to-tree and draped on the side of the house. Everywhere a car could be parked was one—a sea of black polished chrome. A valet took the keys from Max when he pulled up to the porch, and another helped us out. Once we were vertical, Max lead the way past the front door and into the back yard.

The back had been done up like the front, with more strung lights running among wedding style tents. The tents had been set up to create a dining area, a bar, dance floor. All of which were in use.

Max broke away with Gloria. Without my noticing, Awesus had peeled off from the back of our crowd. Rochelle took my arm in hers, and we went to the closest bar together.

I could hear Max across the grounds greeting people, all sparkle and shine. I kept looking around, wondering if I'd catch a glimpse of Samantha. I imagined which window was hers in the house and if her phonograph played softly in her room.

Rochelle ordered for us both, and we sipped, walking hand in hand again through the ritzy back yard. I didn't see Mr. Hamilton under any of the big tents or trotting around to any of the Casa Loma tunes. It was tough to distinguish exactly for what cause all these suits had been assembled. For all I knew, this was an average Friday night around here.

It was a sight to see, a cross-section of the local set thick enough to roll with the likes of Max and Mr. Hamilton. None of the sod farmers or accountants in town for the summer to see the shows. If these were out-of-towners, then home was The Hamptons or The Cape. If they were locals, then they owned the deed to the Mullaghanee's land and several more like it. Some of the guests acknowledged Rochelle as we made our way to the dance floor, which I deftly skirted for as long as I could until our glasses were empty and taken away by a slick waiter.

The tempo had slowed for a break, and we swayed along, holding on loosely. Rain threatened over the ocean, could be felt in the unseen precipitation that made the air seem thicker. It would never accumulate enough to cause any bother tonight, a layer of mist on the tabletops in the morning.

When the band picked up again, they played for I'm not sure how long. Enough for me to have sweat through Max's son's shirt and vest. To have had three or four more champagne's plus a little bit of whatever was being passed around and once as Rochelle and I locked eyes legs kicking out, bodies jerking to a horn making time all its own, a little yellow pill on the tip of my tongue and then coursing through my veins until the jacket was too much to wear and the vest would shrink when it dried, and the shirt would be tarnished. We danced until the music was over and our ears—forced to acclimate to the lull of the crowd—couldn't be trusted to decipher exactly what was being yelled into them. More champagne and my head had swelled. More smoke with some friends of Rochelle's, and I was complacent, listening as though with understanding to more than one conversation entirely in French. The way they talked made it so nice that I didn't even mind if I heard my name in there more than once.

I heard some other names too. One of which I was told I was sitting and chatting with, Mr. McCoy, a real estate man and okay in my book as he lit me a cigarette from his personal case.

"Canadian," he told me with a bit of drawl, "Ontario. You're used to our southern leaf, tastes like shoe leather."

"I kinda' don't mind the taste. It reminds me of something, not sure what. But I like yours too."

"Nice and diplomatic. That's important in business… in all things…but especially in business. If you're planning on going into business with Max, you should know that of all people… he's the least diplomatic..."

"What is Max's business?"

"You aren't working for him?"

"I get it, he's a bootlegger. But what is he really into?"

"How do you know Max?"

"My friend Richie's uncle Sal."

"You ever spent any time up north… have you ever been to Canada?"

"Not at all."

"Up there in Canada, they have a place called Newfoundland. Right off the coast, an island called St. Pierre… it's practically Greenland… almost a town if you could call it that. Up there, we used to run booze out of France and all over Europe… it went into Detroit, New York, even Mud City. That's how I met Max."

"He's from Chicago?"

"At one point or another."

"I would have guessed he was born in Cambridge, maybe in the library basement at Harvard."

"That sounds about right… he's a bit pedantic…"

"He talks twice as much as you, and I understand less than half of what he's saying. If that's what you're getting at."

"That was always his problem. Lonely guys talk a lot… Max talks to himself and everybody else no matter who's around, lonely or not… he talks."

"You saying it's better to be tight-lipped?"

"It goes both ways. You never saw a guy with a zipper for a mouth get too far in any direction. You can't trust a guy that talks too much, sure. But a guy that doesn't give word-one… I'd keep an eye on him."

"Someone killed my buddy, Richie. That's how I know Max."

"Richie?"

"You knew him?"

"…no."

"You sure you ain't being tight-lipped? I wouldn't be sore. You hardly know me, and I've never been to Newfoundland after all." No answer. "What about, Sal? Richie's uncle."

"I've been running booze as long as you've been alive… I've met a few uncles named Sal."

"This is Salvatore Di Giulio. If he's got the same name as his nephew. But I guess he might not."

"Listen here, son… what do you plan on doing while you're hanging around here with Max?"

He caught the glance at Rochelle.

"That's all well and good. Piece of advise... keep an eye on the mark on the bottle… sometimes the drink runs out before the party's over."

"Are you going to sit there all night, Bill?"

It was a woman about McCoy's age, a little younger. "They're finally playing something I know. Let's dance."

"Excuse me. Remember what I said… mind the bottle. Mind Max too while you're at it."

He stood to go dance, taking the lady around the waist.

In the gap of his absence, I caught Max's eye. I don't know how long he had been there across the yard, staring a hole in the back of Mr. McCoy's head. Surely not as long as it took the never-ending curl of his grin to cross his face.

And though I turned away, I knew he was watching, surrounded by others, involved in deep conversation, separated by a million leaves of grass, smiling a lunatic smile. Or was it that he saw the whole picture and had to flex the routine muscles but for else to cry when he looked over and saw the new stranger in his son's shirttails talking softly behind his back.

The party went on late into the night, the day diffusing into the eastern sky. The guests took off in bunches on foot and then in a row of cars. Before long, there were only a handful of guests left in the backyard. We watched as a team came in on a stake bed truck, parked in the middle of the yard, and started pulling up the dance floor in four-foot sections. Gloria and Rochelle went through what was left of the wine at the bar with a few of the Canadians.

"Want to come inside?" Awesus had been walking across the lawn, taking his time, watching the workers pull up the floor, turning to take a look at the brightening horizon.

"Time to go already?"

"Nah, Max wants you."

"What for?"

"How should I know?"

"You're a fountain of insight, Awes."

He sparked up another ace and offered me a hit, but I took a pass. The night had worn on me, and I was looking forward to a clean drink of water more than anything.

"Come on inside anyway."

"You saying I have to?"

"Don't have to do anything."

I didn't get up, and he didn't leave.

"But you'll see that I do, huh?"

The inside of Hamilton's house was quaint and homey. Nothing like the empty castle Max had furnished for himself. There was a parlor room on the first floor. Unlike Max's, everything was arranged with places for guests to sit in silk and velvet. A couple of hired servants floated around. One of them brought me a tall glass of seltzer with a slice of lime. I nodded my thanks about a thousand times and chugged.

When cigarettes had been passed out and lit, I felt like I could think. The crowd consisted of mostly older men: Mr. McCoy was there, Max too.

There were a couple of older ladies, not done up like Gloria and Rochelle but dressed more like their male counterparts, all creases and business with discerning looks being shot at one another and around the room, evaluating the bloated faces—pink from liquor and last night's shaving—they were forced to do business with for the time being.

Max motioned for me to join him and I did.

"Good morning Joseph. Enjoying yourself? How do you like our celebration?"

"Just fine."

"Everyone says you fit right in. She would never say, but I heard Rochelle has taken quite a liking to you." He glanced at Awesus for verification, which he gave. Max put his hand on my knee. "How do you like the suit? It looks perfectly fitting on you. It was my son's, you know."

"Yeah, you said."

"Did I? I can be a bit loquacious. I know that's true. Lovely boy, like his mother. He moved away from me to Chicago."

"What was in Chicago?"

"Our mutual friends, of course! By the by, have you seen Sal lately?"

"I'm the one who was asking you about Sal."

"Were you?" His hand gripped. He seemed to be searching for the memory. "Ah, yes, you did. Certainly."

Samuel Hamilton came into the room drinking a screwdriver and closed the doors behind him.

The hum of conversation quieted.

Lips on cigs and ice in glasses. I had never spent this much time so close to Hamilton. He came to the Barn occasionally and acknowledged me to the same degree he did all the players, with sweeping congratulations to us all onstage or assembled out in the yard. He had the kind of custom-tailored suit folks like him could afford, with a gold chain running from the breast pocket. His light attire matched his general attitude.

"Did everyone enjoy themselves," he asked, taking in all of the guests. Some people clapped politely, others only smiled back at him. "I won't keep you all too long. I know that you have homes—or boats to get to." Some laughs. "What I'd like to speak to everyone about is change. They say that most people are slow to change—or rebel from it altogether. Can you blame me for tapping the kegs and striking up the band?

"It depends. How large of loan do you need?" A man across the room called out. More laughs than before.

"You're right, Mr. Bronfman, not all of us have transitioned the repeal as tactfully as you have. But for those of you who didn't keep up with the Seagram's—I have a proposition that would ease the pressure on your purses."

"I'm not a dirt farmer, so F.D.R. thinks I'm flush," said a woman who sat behind what must be Mr. Hamilton's own desk.

"That's correct. When you almost lost your shirt in the market, did anyone mind? Now that a bunch of orange pickers need a handout, it's reformations and bailouts for all. Prohibition is over. The banks have failed us. I say if we want a new opportunity, we do what our families have done for generations, make it ourselves." He stood and hollered, "Samantha, can you come in here a moment, please?"

She must have been waiting outside the door because she came in before he could finish talking. She didn't look too thrilled to be awake and being shown off to high society like some blue ribbon winner, but what sparkle was missing from her eyes was made up for by the glittering jewels at the base of her perfectly formed earlobes. She didn't see me at first. She looked into the crowd, feigning eye contact at no one in particular while her father continued to talk.

"...South African sourced radiant DeBeers' alluvial diamonds. As you well know, impossible to find for more than two years."

"So, where did you get them, Hamilton?" I couldn't see who was speaking.

"Mr. Ernest Oppenheimer, whom some of you may know, lent them to me specifically for this demonstration. You see, even though the mines in Angola and the Congo have been closed, Mr. Oppenheimer is sitting on the world's largest reserve of uncut carats... roughly four million."

"And he couldn't give them away if he tried," said the woman behind the desk.

"It's true. The cost of these remarkable pieces this morning is strictly for the birds. But I have faith in the dollar. With or without F.D.R., the times will change again for the better. Where do you want your money when it happens, under your mattress, or invested in a rising market?"

"Is that what you brought us out here for Hamilton," it was Mr. Bronfman again, "to invest in a mine? I could have told you, no, as easily in a letter."

"Then you would have missed out on the best odds your money's ever seen. What if I told you that one of the gems you see on my daughter was created underground over millions of years and the other in a laboratory in a few weeks."

"So it's counterfeit?" Another voice I couldn't see.

"Not quite, the stone in question here is synthetic, crafted in the same manner as a real stone: carbon, heat, and pressure. Max is already prepared to convert the whiskey operation to a synthesizing lab. All we need is enough overhead for reconstruction plus initial investments."

Max stood to join Hamilton. "We all thought prohibition would be the end of an era. Instead, we were all granted a new beginning. Now the economy fails, and do you see naught but the darkest muslin over your eyes? Remove it, I say! From the ashes of depression, I see the brightest new hope for our future, a dazzling future." He almost touched Samantha's ear as he used an open palm to display the jewels once more.

She didn't pay Max any mind. Her eyes had met mine. I could practically see the electric impulses trying to make reason of my presence. Max was doing his thing, rambling on about diamonds returning to ninety-five percent of their original value, flooding the market with untraceable, synthesized diamonds, eventually shorting the whole thing.

Small fries. Who cares.

Samantha left the room without looking back.

I went after her.


"Hey there, Samantha."

"What are you doing here?"

"Max brought me."

"Who's Max?"

"A friend of your father's."

"Why are you wearing a suit?"

"It's Max's son's. I think he died."

"It fits you well. Betsie says you haven't been at the Barn."

"I kind of forgot. Were they pretty mad?"

"They figured you went home, I think... because of Richie."

"Right. Who's playing my part?"

"What part?"

"I mean–"

"It's not as though you had a real part."

"No... I know. I thought–"

"They get a new crew every year, Joe. Lots of boys from Massachusetts come up here, and we never see them again."

"And what about guys from Chicago that wind up shot? You folks all used to that too?"

"People like Richie get hurt all the time where he's from, I imagine. He was a heel, Joe. You were the only one that couldn't see it."

"What about Betsie?"

"My sister can manage herself. She was having some fun and now its over."

"More fun than you know."

She slapped me in the face. A wing brushing past on the way to heaven. I could feel my cheek turning red.

"Betsie can take care of herself. She's already been seeing Danny anyway. Richie's dead, and no one cares, only the bums like you who hung around him."

"And your father. I'd hate to see what happens when the whole town finds out he's nothing but a washed-up bootlegger." She slapped me again. The pleasure of contact was dwindling. "No wonder Sal was poking around here the other day. You sent him away, a guy like him could never have anything to do with daddy, right? Unless daddy's nothing but another crook." This time I felt the sting, and it hurt. "But why should we guess? There's an FBI man been hanging around. I got his card in my pocket. I bet he could put all the pieces together for us. Maybe even save your old man from winding up like Richie. Racketeering isn't that serious, he'd probably only be in jail until he croaked. First booze now diamonds." She hit me a couple more times, but it didn't matter.

"They look great on you, by the way. By the sounds of it, you'll never run out. But incase you do, here's a little more evidence for the grand jury."

I slid one of the irregular smokes out from my pack and took one of her hands in mine. I crushed the dry paper letting the tobacco fall into her palm. The diamond earring plopped out. She looked up at me, brushing away the leaf to hold only the stone.

"I won't tell you the reward I thought I'd get for returning it."

She didn't hit me anymore, didn't say a word.

She clutched the stone in her hand and left the room. I didn't have to see the tears to know she cried them. I could still hear Max yammering on in the next room as Samantha's steps clapped away.

*a case of mistaken identity.*

The morning could not break the shade inside the forest. After a few yards, a dense undergrowth gave way to walkable areas amongst the oak and maple trunks. The glossy bottoms of my shoes slipped across the floor of pine needles.

When I was a little kid, my folks were never both gone from the house longer than it took to go to the market or pick up the mail. If I ever wanted to have anything that felt like privacy, I'd sneak out the back door unannounced and walk to the park at the end of the block.

Past the baseball field, there's a strip of woods separating the park from the neighborhood next to ours. If I walked up into those woods and didn't go too far in either direction, I could lose sight of the houses and park, only to be reminded of the outside world if someone hit a real dinger back on the field or some lady started calling for the kids off the back porch. I'd walk and see how far I could go before the sun was down. Supposedly some older guys had found a dead body out there once.

All I ever found was some empty beer cans and one time a trashy novel with most of the pages torn out.

I went cold when I heard the scream. It was Samantha. I ran through the woods until the ground dropped off in a slope and then half slid, half fell down trying to get my footing as the loose dirt and rocks swept me away.

At first, it looked like Samantha was being attacked by some living part of the forest. She struggled out from under a pile of leaves, arms were gripping at her throat and legs trying to stop her own from kicking violently. She couldn't scream anymore but made suppressed crying noises. I found a tree branch about the size of my arm and swung it at the leaves, making contact with the hard rock that was the back of Sal's head, which split open parallel to his bald hairline loosening the warm red stuff in glugs. His arms let go, and Samantha rolled out from under him, blood smeared over her face and clothes. Sal slumped over on his side. I got Samantha up on her feet. I put my suit jacket around her shoulders and used the handkerchief from the breast pocket to wipe her face. Her neck was already starting to bruise. She was shaken and paler than hell but otherwise seemed alright.

"Can you walk?"

She nodded. I helped her up the embankment and watched as she stumbled back the way we came.

I could hear Sal's attempts to breathe when I got close to him again. The blood had already pooled around him, wetting the leaves, matting his hair. I had to squat to roll him over. By the time I had him on his back, I was covered in his blood.

He had been shot four or five times.

The open wounds in his chest gurgled as he tried to continue pumping oxygen. His eyes fluttered. Closed. Opened again.

He didn't look like he was in much pain.

"Wuh…wallet." His lips were sticking together.

I sat down next to him and dug inside his pockets until I pulled out a brown leather wallet. Inside was the average stuff: cash, driver's identification, a picture of a lady about Sal's age. He grasped at the wallet, guiding me to a tack-sewn compartment in the back. I tore it open to reveal a waxed card identifying Sal as a federal agent.

Name: Solomon Tappinger
Investigator — FBI

The back of the card contained what was almost a phone number and then a long string of numbers and letters. The only other thing in the compartment was a piece of paper no larger than a dime, rough in texture, stained a little pink. Sal fumbled around until the scrap stuck to one of his bloodied fingers. He stuck his finger in his mouth and with a great deal of effort swallowed. I didn't look at him again, but when he reached his hand out, I took it in mine and held on until his breathing stopped, which wasn't that long.

*

The woods turned out to be less deep than I expected. I came across a dirt path barely wide enough for a vehicle which I followed for a piece until there was a dugout with a car pulled off into it, Sal's car. The windows were rolled down, the keys left in the front seat. There weren't any other identifying materials inside the glove box or anywhere else. In the trunk was a plain suitcase with a spare set of clothes, some shaving stuff, and a bottle of booze Sal must have pinched from Max's. I got in and started it up and backed out until I found another dugout to turn around in. The path lead to a road I had never been on. I tugged on the booze and lit up, going toward the sun to get to the coast. I pulled into Ogunquit before noon and found myself parked between Richie's and a pay telephone.

"Operator. To whom may I direct your call?"

I read the first row of digits from Sal's waxed card to the woman. I could hear her talking to someone on the other end.

Then a new voice, "Could you repeat that, please, sir?"

I did.

"Connecting now."

There was a series of static clacks as wires were plugged in and out of ports. A few bells and tones later and I was listening to a third woman's voice.

"Please report."

"Umm…"

"Your credentials."

"Solomon Tappinger."

"Your authorization."

I rattled off the longer string of numbers and letters.

"Good day, Agent Tappinger. Are you in need of extraction?"

"My name is Joe Burke. I got this number from Sal's– well, Mr. Tappinger's wallet. He showed me where it was."

"Where is Agent Tappinger?"

"He's dead. I killed him. Well, he was shot, but I hit him after he woke up with a tree branch. But then he ate some drugs or something out of his wallet. I'd say that's what killed him."

A few moments passed in silence.

"You're quite sure he's deceased?"

"Pretty sure."

"Your name?"

"Joe Burke," I told her again.

"Your location?"

I read her the address off the phone booth.

"Do you have any of Tappinger's belongings?"

"Nothing but the card I used to call you and his car."

"Listen to me carefully, Mr. Burke. You are in possession of federal property. Upon my authority, I demand that you destroy any articles of identification related to Tappinger, including but not limited to license, photos, written, or recorded communiqué. Do you understand?"

"What if I need to contact you again?"

"Under no circumstance should you attempt to contact this office again. Do you understand?"

"I get it." I cradled the earpiece and lit a match, holding it under the credentials with my free hand. The wax dripped and turned black, then the paper was lit and burned up in my hand.

"Leave the vehicle at your current location with the keys and Agent Tappinger's wallet in the front seat. An extraction team will be dispatched shortly."

"I don't have his wallet."

"You said he gave it to you."

"He showed it to me. I didn't take it from him."

Again with the silence.

"How far is Agent Tappinger from your location?"

"He's a few miles from here. In the woods."

"Mr. Burke, are you of sound body and mind?"

"I suppose."

"Are you willing and able to complete a task which I assign?"

"Sure."

"You have my permission to continue using Tappinger's vehicle in order to retrieve his credentials and any other identifying materials. Are you able to lift the body?"

"I don't know, lady. Have you ever met Sal… er… Tappinger?"

"You cannot lift him?"

"I cannot."

"Then you are to proceed with the utmost caution to retrieve his credentials and any other identifying materials including but not limited to license, photos, communiqué, jewelry, or anything which seems of importance."

"Should I check for fillings?"

"The extraction team will handle that when they arrive." She was a real sport. "If all goes well, an agent will make contact with further instructions."

"Wallace?"

"I'm sorry?"

"Will I make contact with Wallace?"

"Who is Wallace?"

"He's one of your guys."

She was quiet for longer this time.

When she came back she spoke more intently.

"There is no agent Wallace on record in your area. This man approached you?"

"A couple of times."

"And you told him…"

"Squat. He's a creep."

"But you spoke with him. What about?"

"He wanted to know about Richie and the diamonds."

"Who is Richie?"

"Richie Di Giulio. I thought he was Sal's nephew. I guess I don't know who he is."

"You've been in contact with the Di Giulios?"

"One of them at least."

"And now you have their diamonds."

"Hamilton's diamonds, but I gave them back to Samantha. Agent Tappinger was choking her when I hit him."

I only spoke to the woman for another few minutes. After hearing me out, she had instructed me to use Tappinger's vehicle to go back to his body and retrieve his credentials, which I was in the process of doing.

I was about a tank of gas away from headed home and calling it quits on the whole summer and everything.

I parked the Imperial in the spot I found it and passed on foot through the dangling leaves and spider webs. Sal's body was still there. The body which had once belonged to Sal. The body which had once been named Sal by another. It was a pity to look at. I still kind of thought of him as Richie's uncle.

The wallet was in the leaves by the body.

I took it.

"Why don't you come back to the house?" Awesus was standing on the edge of the embankment, looking down on me crouched next to Sal's lifeless body.

I squinted up at him. "Tell you the truth, I don't feel much like going anywhere. What's back at the house you want me to see so bad?"

"Nothing to see. Party's over."

"I suppose I'll be getting along then."

"We're going along. Back to Max's. How's that sound?"

"Just fine."

\*

The few cars that remained for Max's sales pitch had gone, leaving only his roadster parked in the front yard. Awesus lead me from the foyer to the study, where Max waited with Hamilton.

"There's my boy," Max said, taking me in his arms. Taking no notice of the blood on my shirt front. He held me to him by one shoulder. Hamilton had taken up his seat at his desk. He was rather pale, and if I didn't know better, I'd say he had been crying. His tie was gone, top button unbuttoned. He didn't seem to remember the long, western-movie type revolver clasped in his right hand and kept waving it around loosely as he spoke.

"They'll be coming any time now. You know that, don't you?"

"We really did enjoy ourselves, Samuel." Max paid no mind to the flailing gun. Hamilton continued as without hearing. "And now, there are witnesses. You had to put on a big show!"

"Accomplices of a separate class. Our family in Chicago wouldn't even know where to start asking."

"What about Bronfman? McCoy? They all talk."

"About hooch, not diamonds. McCoy's a straight shooter and now that the ban is lifted, he'll probably skitter away down to Florida. Same with Bronfman… he's in a legitimate business as of now. If Sal's people call, he won't even answer the phone. Let alone sell us out."

"Sal's people… oh God."

He was on the verge of bawling.

"What the hell are we supposed to say about Sal?"

"Never saw him. Heard he's a fine gent."

"But they'll know, Max. People like that always know those things. It's a part of life for them. Not like you and me."

"No one knows better than I what they're capable of! Lest you force me to remind you."

"I wish I never met him. Or you for that matter."

"Come now, Samuel. We're friends. We must stick together. Mustn't let business get between friends. Friends 'til the end."

"Would you shut up."

"You're upset. I understand. You and your daughter have been through a great deal these last two days."

"Leave my daughter out of this."

"Too late for that, isn't it?"

Hamilton looked up at Max.

"I should say you killed him. That's why he was here, you know. You're next on the list. Teach some dullard how to make cheap liquor, and we could have been finished with you years ago."

79

"If you really want to look like a star, why not kill us now and do everyone a favor?" Max stepped forward.

"Don't think I wouldn't."

The gun was leveled. In the same instant, Awesus crossed the room, laid his palm across the barrel, and jerked it from Hamilton's grip. Hamilton stood, but Awesus pushed him back down. Hamilton stood again, and Awesus punched him right below the ribs. That kept him down as he tried to catch his breath.

"What am I to do," choking for air, "I'm digging a hole, and they're filling it in behind me. How much longer before it's my grave, Max? How much deeper can I go?"

Max crouched next to the desk, looking up at Hamilton, "There's no end to that well, the dirt of which is exhumed from the most private and supple places of your being. You should send your girls away from here. To their mother's."

"They would hate that."

"More than the alternative?"

"What about him?" Hamilton acknowledged my blood-stained presence for the first time.

"You let me worry about my boy."

The ride to Max's was quiet and less death-defying than last night. Max drove and continued drinking. I'm guessing he never took a break. Awesus sat in the back, toking on another in a long line of funny sticks. Neither offered me nothing of anything, and I wouldn't have wanted it if they did. I wanted to get back to the house and get changed out of these damn clothes and take a shower and scrub the blood off my skin where it had soaked through the cloth.

There were no other cars parked in the drive when we got to the house. The front door was open. Max walked right in as though that were perfectly normal. He didn't take notice of the broken vase knocked over in the main hall. He didn't seem to mind that his study was trashed. Liquor and glass splattered all over. What did seem to bother him was that the curtains in each room had been torn down.

The drapes hung tattered.

Daylight revealed the results of the past.

The stain from a leaking pipe down the wallpaper.

A crack in the glass of a ceiling-height window.

The chipped paint on the raised panels of the doors.

I went from one room to another and upstairs looking for Rochelle. The doors were open up there too. Bare windows illuminating years of dust.

I passed what must have been Gloria's room.

Empty.

Next was Max's room, velvety and grand, if it weren't for the musty pillars of books that remained stacked here and there. Many had been knocked over and strewn around, torn with pages spilling out like guts.

The sunlight was the worst in here.

Brightest shining stark indifference.

Two more rooms down was Rochelle's. Nothing had changed much in there. The curtains drawn aside but not ripped down.

Her clothes packed without a big show.

The bed was made, books aligned on the night table.

My clothes were folded on the vanity with a note pinned to my jeans.

*Joe,*

*I could not leave without saying goodbye. When I first met Max I thought he was my brother. We were raised under one roof but we are not family unless that is the only condition. His mother and father were both brilliant. They are the ones who worked with Moissan. He had many failures and learned many lessons. There are no books that mention them, the lab assistants determined to outshine through synthetics the attempts of their master, or my father who fought for liberty in Champagne and who hunted and trapped and washed the floors of a chemistry laboratory so that his daughter might have a new dress to wear and meat other than venison to eat. He was there when the furnace exploded. He knew Max's parents well and he died trying to pull their bodies from the flames. Max is a good man but he mustn't be trusted. He has had his family taken from him more than once and I fear what may happen to him when I leave but I have to go for myself. Gloria is the closest chance I have for family aside from him and I must follow her now if I have any chance to find if I can love. I won't tell you where we will go. He may find this and try to follow. I'll only say that you are a very sweet boy and I wish that I had never met you.*

*summer's almost gone*
*the sun rose so late today*
  *flame he can't shut out*

*I'm sorry about your friend Richie.*
  *-Rochelle*

A drawer opened in a room where I had never been. I could hear the rustling around of clothes and shoes as I hid the letter away and crept out into the hall. I looked in the door which had almost been closed, but not all the way. Awesus was standing with his back to me, stripped down to his shorts. His body was pale as his face but had been marked all over by intricate tattoos from forearm to ankle. Most of the ink was in patterns of lines and dots with some images woven in. An eagle with outspread wings soared between his shoulder blades. I wouldn't doubt the power of the guy, but his body revealed an age that you'd never see in his face. Deep creases in the fat above his hips, excess skin around his shoulder blades. All of the places that were once taught and firm had been pulled earthward over time, softened by fine cooking and financial security. He turned to face me, revealing scar tissue from navel to collar bone. The tattoos resumed around the edges of his ribs and stomach, but none had survived in the burned area, and he had made no effort to replace them. He walked over when he saw me and closed the door.

*

The blood ran pink, then clear, then out the drain. It felt good to have it off me. I put my jeans and shirt on and found my shoes and socks by the bed. Downstairs the covers had been returned to the windows in at least one room. I found Max in his study with a lamp, working on his translation. He had changed into a set of silk pajamas and a dressing gown and smoked a pipe, hair combed back, looking nothing like

83

a guy who had a piece stuck at him early in the morning. He sipped from a coffee and motioned to the liquor cabinet where a silver pot waited with ceramic dishes. I didn't pour myself a cup.

"I wanted to thank you for all the swell times," I told him. "It's been a real pleasure to be your guest. I'm gonna be going now. Gonna head back to the Barn, they might be wondering what happened." He kept scratching away in his notebook. "Well, so long." I walked to the door snatching a souvenir from the liquor cabinet that hadn't been caught up in Gloria's rampage.

Max's voice interrupted my exit.

"What if a person was better than they were meant to be? If someone is responsible and kind and giving, are they lifted into a higher state of being… or simply put upon more by themselves to do what is perceived as good… convincing others it's true? Do all others look, and think of holding themselves to that standard… the golden rule. Or do they rebel more, thinking that the good one has thrown the curve? Would that offset the balance of all those responsible and kind and giving things? Were we ever really meant to be good at all?"

"You talking about yourself?"

He took the pipe from his mouth. "No, Joseph… I'm none of those things. Can you think of a person who could be held to that standard?"

"Did you want me to start naming them?"

"That isn't necessary."

Awesus joined us or had been standing there a while, I wasn't sure which. I couldn't shake the vision of him as older and saw it on him even now.

"They never attained the desired results."

"You think you can?"

"I'm sure of it, Joseph. We don't only have the benefit of modern facilities, we also have access to the most valuable lesson we could desire... the failures of our predecessors."

"If it's all the same to you, I'd rather not be here when you learn this one."

"You'd like... to leave?"

"You better believe it."

"Would you like Awesus to drive you back to the Barn?"

"I don't need nothing else from you. Thanks for everything."

I left how I came, heading for the front entrance blocked by a man who, if he had hinges, would have made a great door. I could see the broken lines of his face despite the shadow from the afternoon sun. Wallace entered, looking madder than the .38 gripped in his palm.

"Where's Max?"

"Back there." I hiked my thumb over my shoulder.

"That bastard around?" I didn't answer that one.

"He's always around. He got a piece with him?"

"How should I know?"

"He always does. Okay, kid. Lead the way."

I took him through the shattered ballroom. Max was seated in his easy-chair when we got to the study. If Awesus was packing, he didn't show it.

"Pour us a drink." Wallace motioned to the bottle I had forgotten I was carrying. I poured glasses and brought one to Wallace. Max had his own already. Awesus drifted closer, putting himself between Max and the gun, didn't take his eyes off Wallace, who didn't take his eyes off Max.

"You got a lot to answer for, you know that?" Wallace drank.

"I have some questions for you myself," said Max.

"You're gonna answer for what you done."

"Did you know my Helena?"

Wallace emptied his glass. "Of course, I did. It's a miracle you didn't get snubbed out a long time ago after what you did to her."

"Loved her? Help me to refresh my memory, dear friend. I've allowed you into my home… shared my drink. The least you could do is help stir my nostalgia. Is love her what I did to earn the pleasure of your so welcomed personage alighted under my arches?"

"Can the dramatics. You know what you done. Screwing around with Netti is like screwing around with the boss."

"I was simply doing what was best for my family."

"I'm sorry about your boy and about Helena. But that's in the past. You gotta' pony up where it's due. Boss's rules, not mine."

"Where is it due? What's owed? Last time the chits were balanced, it was I who was owed."

"I ain't gonna argue with you, pal. We both know how it stands. Give me the diamonds. Any you got. Any you made. Any the kid has or what he gave to his little girlfriend."

"I haven't produced stone one. Do you want me to surrender the stills? My home? I've given my family. My loved ones taken not once, but four times. Mother… father… lover… son. What else would you take, my life? There's nothing else I'd more gladly part withal… do you recognize that, Joseph?"

Max reached out, abruptly standing and putting his arm on my shoulder. I half expected him to shoot me. What he did was probably worse. He began to sob uncontrollably. The tears wetted the cloth on my shoulder. He dropped the glass he was holding. More shards on the floor.

Wallace finished his drink. "Leave the diamonds and hooch and all that stuff in the basement and get out."

Max spun to face him. "I've told you already I don't have any damned diamonds. Hamilton has the presentation pieces. That's all there is. If your boss wants to try his hand at elemental physics, be my guest."

"He does then," Wallace motioned at me. "He's got the stash Richie got from Hamilton."

"From Hamilton?"

"He's got them someplace in that Barn."

"What stash does he mean," he asked me.

"Hamilton's been arranging distribution for Oppenheimer," Wallace told him. "They'll run the market as soon as FDR pulls us all out of the dumper."

"Hamilton is doing this?" Max's neck bulged against his collar. "I don't know what bull they've been shoveling on you, but this is true. They got DeBeers people in on it too. Ad campaigns."

"Hamilton?" Max asked again.

"You're done, pal. No one needs a bootlegger. The boss is turning this place into a country house."

"This is my home. Close the operation, but you can't have my home."

"Ain't yours no more. It belongs to the family, and they ain't your family no more either. Me and the kid are going to the Barn to get that stash. Then I'm coming back with a few tough buddies to do some inventory. You'll be gone by then."

Wallace put his free hand over my shoulder, kept the .38 on Awesus, pulled me out into the ballroom. Max collapsed into his easy-chair, pounding his fists on the arms. Awesus stayed where he was. Wallace didn't turn until we had reached the front door. As we spun, Max drove one hand beneath his seat cushion and sprang to his feet. There was no sound of Max's house slippers on the polished marble.

No shouting or scuffle.
The shots cracked in quick succession.
A midday breeze rustled the leaves in the yard.
A chickadee called out bravely once to no reply. When his trill let out again, the world resumed a usual state of affairs.
Max waited, draped in gun smoke. He pushed his hair back several times, assuming correctly that it was very out of place.
The .38 hit the floor. Wallace's mangled arm drooped to his side. The shots had torn right through him in a couple places. He was missing most of his shoulder and neck on the right side. Another pulsing divot had opened his shirt-front.
Shiny glandular ooze sucked in and out as he tried to breathe, his insides running over the front of his pants.
He looked down to inspect his wounds and let out a mouthful of thick black blood. He straightened up and walked drunkenly out of the ballroom, out the front door, and down the steps.

Awesus took the pistol from Max and handed him a fresh drink. Max fell into his chair, spilling a little booze on his shirt sleeve. Awesus followed after Wallace, scooping up the fallen revolver.

"Joseph! Come have a drink." Max hollered from his seat.

I went to the kitchen and dug Wallace's business card out of my pocket, crumpled it up and threw it away.

"Joseph! Come now, son. I didn't hurt you, did I!"

I used the kitchen phone to call The Hack, who answered after so long I had to ask the operator to try him twice.


"What are you doing in here?" Max said when I hung up. He leaned in the narrow doorway, sloshing the remnants of his booze and ice.

"Calling my mother. It's her birthday today."

"What a nice boy. How old is dear mother?"

"You know, I'm not sure? Pretty old."

"How nice. Do you have any siblings?"

"Nope."

"Ever been to a funeral?"

"A few. Relatives."

"What about your friend Richie?"

"Hasn't been a funeral yet. That's why Sal came to town."

"Is that why you really think Sal came to visit?"

"No."

"Do you know what Sal is?"

"Was," I reminded him. "Does Hamilton know?"

"How could I be sure? Regardless, he's right to be afraid. Do you really have the diamonds?"

I took out the remaining gem laden stick and pulled the filter off before lighting up. I peeled the paper off the cotton and removed the stone, handing it over to Max.

"And there are more?"

"Some. A lot, I mean. I mean, there must be even more than I saw."

"Yes, there must. A stockpile. You'll have to get what you have and bring them here."

"Are you going to give them to Wallace?"

"I'm going to leave them here like he asked."

"Where will you go?"

"I'm not sure, but Wallace and his friends are dangerous people, and I'm very tired of being associated with them."

"They killed your son, huh?"

"Yes, Joseph, they did."

"And your wife?"

"Helena? No, never. She blamed me for letting him move to Chicago, but she blamed herself more for her blood. She couldn't let herself get away with it."

"Did you kill Richie?"

Max set the diamond down and finished his glass.

"I did not kill Richie," he said so it must have been true. He pocketed the diamond and stood aside to let me pass.

"How do you know I'll come back?"

"You're a good boy. I know you will make me nothing short of proud... Awesus will drive you there and back."

Awesus was silent the whole drive. Didn't smoke his funny sticks, didn't take the bottle when I offered some from the one I had snatched. I asked him to pass the Barn entrance and hang down the way a little. He found a spot and killed the engine. I got out and walked a very familiar stretch of dirt leading up to the Barn. A road I had walked every night for months. A rut whose path was dug by the soles of my shoes. Same person, same shoes, same rut. Worn away, dirt and rubber and something human, not changed.

The lights were off in the house, and the Barn was closed up. The hay bale shadows slept in the field. A restless chicken pecked around the pen by the coop. Up late, pacing. She could probably use a smoke and a stiff drink. I walked the long way to the back of the Barn, making sure no one was lurking around. I went all the way to shed and looked in through a glass pane. My cot was there with my extra clothes. A layer of sawdust covered everything like fresh snow. They probably cut down the cherry blossom tree to make way for the Pinafore's brass-work. So what? Wallace's buddies would dunk me and Max and Awes in concrete somewhere. Cornerstones in some real swank downtown high rises.
Just fine.

The door to the back of the Barn was unlocked when I got to it. It had been a couple days since I had been back stage, and I banged my shin more than once getting out into the theatre. I could tell in the dim light that the tree had not actually been removed. I set the bottle down and took out the back panel of my hiding spot. The stash had not been disturbed. I rolled the stones around inside the pouch.

A fortune of death in my palm. I pocketed the stash and closed up the panel and habitually rolled the tree onto its opening mark.

I was almost offstage when Betsie appeared from the wings. I couldn't tell if she was drunk, but she was a mess for sure. Done up with ribbons and bows as always, but her face was haggard and dry, eyes bloodshot, lips swollen—chewing on her lowest, her chin working to stifle a sob which came anyway. She wiped her face with the sleeve of her fancy dress, sniffled, walked to center stage, finding where the moon shone.

Diamonds glinted in her ears.

Grey steel flashed in her hand.

The silken robe wrapped around her, slightly undone, but she didn't move to close it. The cloth fluttered around her bare waist as she swayed on her mark. The gun danced around in the sheen of fine thread. I was only feet away, but she didn't notice. Her feet stuttered out some learned step she didn't seem to be aware of to music only she was aware of.

"Hey there, Betsie."

"Joe! Shouldn't you be getting ready? Where is everyone?"

"Everyone's gone. Were you in the show?"

"The show hasn't started. Where is everyone? They'll be late."

"Have you been home tonight?"

"That's where I came from. Me and Samantha."

"Where's Samantha?"

"Back stage with the others getting ready."

"I got a car waiting outside. Why don't I get you a lift."

Her gaze was sharpened by some remembering she apparently did not want to be doing.

"That's where I came from, silly. I'm not going back."

"You have to. Then you'll go to your mother's"

"Mother?"

"Yeah. You and Samantha. I'm gonna take you home, then you're gonna take Samantha to your mother's."

"And daddy?"

"He has some really important stuff to do, so you gotta take care of your sister. Can you do that and take her away for a little while… to your mother's?"

"Is he going away?" Tears were forming.

"He's not going anywhere. You are."

"Are you taking me?"

"You're taking your sister."

"He said they'd never take me. He'd never let me go."

"No one's getting taken, okay? You're leaving for a while, and then you'll come back, and daddy will be there, and everything will be just fine. Get it?"

"They tried to take him from me already, but I stopped them."

"Stopped who?"

"That FBI man. He came to the house… he said he knew daddy, and he said he knew Richie and you."

"Did they talk?"

"Yes. In daddy's study."

"What about?"

"I'm not sure."

"Does your daddy– Mr. Hamilton know? He knows Sal's a fed?"

"After a while, I went to check in on them. He was leading daddy out the front door with a gun, he had his hands cuffed.

They didn't hear me go into the study. They were almost at the car when I got outside. The man hid his gun when he saw me coming…"

"Have you talked to anyone about this?"

"Samantha doesn't know."

"Not Samantha! Anyone else? Wallace?"

"I don't know. I don't know who that is."

"It doesn't matter. You have to get changed. And take those rocks out of your ears."

Her free hand went up defensively.

"I got these from Richie."

I stepped toward her, the gun backed me off.

"The show's over, Betsie."

I tried to move as Awesus would.

Covered the gap between us in a flash cutting sideways.

I got my hands on the barrel, but she wrenched it free.

Finger on the trigger. The barrel exploded.

Barnwood confetti. Gunpowder fog.

Three slugs from a six-shot gun.

Two would already be in Sal's chest.

Two in the walls.

One below my shoulder.

Betsie collapsed. The piece skidded away.

The cherry blossom tree wavered and blurred. I knelt next to her on the ground cradling my limp appendage in my lap. My upper arm looked like a dog had ripped a mouth-sized chunk out of it.

Betsie was hysterical, calling out, "I killed him!" between fits of tears. Kneeling beside her, I managed to get the sash off her costume with my right hand and wrapped it around my left arm. I threw the sash over my shoulder and wrapped my arm up to my chest, tightening the knot with my teeth. Betsie had taken my advice and begun to get changed—a wrack of skin and robes pinwheeled on the floor.

All kinds of noises were coming from the farmhouse, footsteps, and doors, and stairs. I found an overcoat on a costume rack and covered her with it, pulling away the lacy stuff which had wrapped around her bare feet, ruining the fabric with my blood. I shouldered my way into another coat and stuffed her gun into one of the pockets.

The noises were coming from the dooryard now, the Barn was being opened. I grabbed the bottle, got Betsie up, and half walked, half dragged her into the wings.

The lights were up all around the farmhouse. Some people that I knew but couldn't make out by their silhouettes were running across the yard. I took Betsie around the back of the shed and far side of the property so that we avoided the driveway all together.

We came out to the road a ways down from where Awesus was still parked. Headlamps flashed and died.

The Hack was waiting, half pulled into the bushes on the road-side. He jumped out of the car and helped me put Betsie in the backseat. I slumped against the frame, almost dropped the bottle, but The Hack snagged it and tossed it in the front seat. He tossed me in after the bottle. I drank a couple times and gave it to him.

"You know where the Hamilton place is?"

"Sure enough." He started the car and took off.

The farm was all commotion.

Lanterns and flashlights searched for what they didn't know was us as we passed by. Betsie had quieted down and was breathing peacefully, laid out in the back. I removed the sack of diamonds from my jeans, and tucked it inside one of the more aptly sized pockets of the coat. The Hack glanced at the bag but didn't mention it.

Turns out he was from here and knows most of the folks who built the house in Elliot before Max's family had ever moved to these parts. He knew about the Barn and the Hamilton family. He knew the family that owned the Barn before Hamilton and knew some of the guys who came to reap it every year.

"Some years if there's a wet summah, the rain can get to the bales before they ever get a chance to cure. Lose a whole crop that way... a'course out west they got the exact opposite problem. Sometimes whole valleys will go dry for years at a time. Crops dry out. Animals die off. People pack up and move back to where they came from. Some of them don't have any place else to go, and they die right after the cows. It's a hard road living off the land. There's no will to nature's temperament. The pagans out west dance and kill animals and make love for the rain. Around here, I notice folks do all the same but not usually in the name of anything, rain or shine."

"They're not all exactly living off the land either."

"Whatever you're telling me, I don't want to know it."

"You could suppose as much as there is."

"Let's keep it that way."

He drove steadily with both hands on the wheel except for when he reached to take a nip off the bottle. Though he drank often, the bottle would have lasted him days, and each sip must have only been enough to coat the tongue and gums before being absorbed.

"I've had too much swill too quick. Gotta savor the good stuff while you got it. It's not every day you meet a friend' the family, and a kind one at that."

"Quit saying that will you. My family's not that big, and they aren't from Chicago."

"A friend in some regard says the liquor and that bandage on your arm."

"All my friends are dead."

"Sorry to hear it."

"Don't be. There weren't that many to begin with."

"What about her?" He regarded Betsie through the rearview.

"I don't know. What do you say, Bets? Now that Richie's gone, we still got any reason to be friends?"

Betsie's hand brushed past over the back of the seat. She dropped two glinting stones in my lap. I scooped them up and turned to her as much as I could. Her starry-eyes, all I could find of her when the light would allow, fading before the fall. For her, the leaves of autumn had already turned and dropped. For her, the early nighttime bleakness of winter was the coat she would wear, determined to never see spring again, or the solstice pass which brings the most flourishing times, and eager boys and girls truck in from out of state to be lost for three months dreaming of one day being found.

"Hey, Betsie?"

"Yeah, Joe."

"You didn't kill Richie, did you?"

She drew the fur collar up around her face, almost disappearing in the overcoat. She had tears left to cry for him, and I wouldn't blame her if she threw in a few for herself.

*which way did they go?*

Samantha hadn't been gone long by the time we got to the Hamilton's. The Andrews Sisters were still singing upstairs when I went inside. The lights were on. The house was clean and neat. There was a note on the kitchen counter:

*Betsie,*
*I went to mother's*
*I'll see you there. Daddy says you should come*
*He'll be gone on business for a few days*

*- Samantha*

I read it a couple times then stuffed it in my pocket. I didn't spend much time looking around. The record stopped playing but kept spinning. The needle thumped along the inner label, asking to be carried home. The Hack was waiting at the end of the drive, smoking. Betsie was curled up in the back, asleep. The Hack had got an old blanket out of his trunk to cover her.

He offered me a smoke, and I took it.

"Gone?" He asked.

"Yeah."

"Where to?"

"She went to the mother's"

"Know where that is?"

A pair of headlights appeared down the road before I could tell him I didn't. We got in the cab and watched as a blacked-out four-door crept to a halt. It didn't pull up the driveway, sat there idling not fifty feet away from us.

"Is that the father's car?" The Hack studied his side-view mirror, trying to get a better look through the brake light exhaust.

"That's not daddy." Betsie had poked up her head enough to see out the back window.

"Is it your mother?"

"Mother lives in Connecticut. She never comes here."

She slumped down into the seat again. The brake lights went off, and the car began to roll away as smoothly as it came.

"Can I have a smoke," Betsie asked. "My head is really hurting."

"I'm fresh out," I told The Hack.

He got her one and asked, "You want to follow after them?"

"Nah. There's a diner open late on the other side of town."

*

We took back roads to The Miss Ogunquit diner. Betsie had a couple of tugs from the bottle with us and the drink was close to gone when The Hack got it back in his hands.

"You owe me another." He screwed on the cap.

"I probably owe you a case."

Betsie was okay to walk inside by the time we parked.

"My god, your arm," she said when my coat was brushed aside on the way up the steps, "what happened?"

"An accident."

She went to the restroom to straighten up. Vicky was behind the counter and recognized me when I took a seat on a stool.

"Was that Betsie Hamilton?"

"Yeah."

"Where's your other friend?"

"He doesn't have any friends."

The Hack took a seat beside me.

"Who does that make you then, mister?"

"That makes me Ronald Lloyd or plain old Lloyd if you like. And who might you be if you don't mind me asking?"

"My name's Vicky, and it's my pleasure to tell you."

They shook hands. Ronald Lloyd: hack driver, small towner, good stuff boozer by the thimbleful. He filled the time with so many memories that I never thought to ask him much, especially not about himself. The stories that he told painted a picture of what I assumed must be his personality but would probably never know.

Betsie came out all fixed up but still looking pretty shaky. Vicky poured her a cup of coffee over the counter.

"Who's hungry? My treat." Vicky announced.

The three of us drank coffee while Vicky cooked. Betsie used the phone behind the counter to make a call to her mother's. It turned out mother had no idea Samantha was on her way, but she wouldn't know yet because mother was all the way down in Connecticut, and no one had told her. She was happy to have Betsie come there and would have a car sent as soon as she could. Judging the distance and time of night they decided it would take at least four hours for a car to arrive and Vicky hollered from the kitchen, "That's okay she can wait here with me," and it was decided that Betsie would wait there for a ride to her mother's and hopefully in that time mother would call back and let her know that Samantha had arrived there safely. While we ate biscuits, Vicky busied herself cleaning until interrupted by the opening of the front door.

Two men entered wearing tailored suits and hats to match. One of them, a broad guy. The other, tall and lanky. They shuffled in, letting the door snap closed on the spring behind them. Skinny hung back while the Big Guy approached the counter.

"You work here?" Big Guy asked.

"If you can call it that." Vicky wiped at the counter.

"You live around here then?"

"You boys gonna order anything?"

Big Guy looked over his shoulder at Skinny. "We're a little lost. Looking for a town called Elliot."

"Don't know it, mister. At least have some coffee. How about your friend?"

"We don't need nothin' but directions."

"I'm a waitress, not a tour guide. You need directions, phones on the wall. You're welcome to use it for a dime."

Big Guy turned around, walking over to Skinny, "Phone's on the wall, she says. You believe this shit?"

"Buncha' hicks, whaddya expect?"

"Yeah," Big Guy opened the door and started to walk out.

Skinny followed, "What now?"

"Let's go turn over the Hamilton joint. He must have something says where to find–"

When Betsie's breath caught in her throat, she almost choked. Big Guy stopped halfway out the door. We all turned to look at Betsie, who was holding back all but a few tears.

"What's her problem," Big Guy asked.

No one told him.

"Something's friggin' zooey in here, and I want to know what it is."

"Went down the wrong pipe is all. Never you mind." Vicky was bringing a cup of water to Betsie, who did her best to sip at it despite a sudden onset of the shakes.

"Why's she crying?"

"Why you so funny looking? I told you once to mind yours."

The Big Guy looked funnier than ever trying to get that one through his head. Skinny put a hand on his shoulder, but Big Guy charged the bar. Lloyd stood to block Vicky from him. The Big Guy was big, but Lloyd had a taut kind of farm strength.

"The girl's upset," Lloyd told him, "young love, you know. She and my son here called it off tonight."

"Summer romance. I get it. Been a while, but I get it." Big Guy pushed his gaze down at me from under his shelf of a forehead, "Heartbreaker, huh, kid? Don't break 'em all too soon."

"They were raising hell so bad at home the missus told me to take them out and make 'em civil or not come back."

The Big Guy whistled through his teeth. "Boy, that's a chore.

Do the old man a favor, kids. Kiss and make up so he can go get some winks." He patted Lloyd on the shoulder as he left, "Good luck, pal."

Skinny opened the door, and they both went out with another smack of the wood frame. Betsie buried her face in her hands. Vicky came around from the kitchen and put a CLOSED sign on the door before locking it and going to stand next to Betsie, holding her around the shoulders, brushing her hair aside and rocking with her as she cried short gasping cries.

*spurious.*

Vicky agreed to keep the diner closed until Betsie was picked up. Then she'd call the police from a pay telephone and tell them there had been trouble out at Hamilton's.

"I'll probably call it a night after that. Unless you're thinking of heading back this way?"

I told her I wasn't sure and thanked her and we left.

Lloyd and me polished off what was left of the booze on our way to Max's. With Big Guy and Skinny headed off toward Hamilton's, I figured I'd have a chance to at least give Max a heads-up.

"Seems to me like you done enough already," Lloyd weighed in as we got close to the Maine border. "Don't see why you don't let those boys from the diner take care of their business and let the cops take care of the rest."

"That's one idea."

"Still a chance, you know. If you want, we could turn it right around and take those diamonds to the police back in town. They'd make sure everything turned out right for you."

"Probably would. You got any more smokes?"

"Ayuh." He handed me one.

They probably would take care of me, Captain Montgomery and his boys. Once the feds got to town, they'd take care of Big Guy, Skinny, Hamilton, and any other missing pieces. Then they'd take care of Max—or what was left of him. Max, the bootlegger who, as far as I could tell, had never done much wrong except marry into the wrong family and shoot a guy no one liked too much in the back. If you asked me, Max was the next best thing to okay, and right now, I had his salvation bouncing against my thigh.

"Do me a favor," I asked Lloyd.

"You get me another of them good bottles, and you got anything you need."

"After you drop me, can you spin around back to the diner? Keep an eye on those two."

"You bet."

I had him let me out at the end of Max's driveway.

"Give me a call if you need a lift. And don't forget my bottle."

No lights were visible inside the house when I emerged onto Max's sprawling front yard. He must have spent some time re-covering all the windows. The house stood out against the night sky only enough to make out the most simple form, a blotch on the horizon gaining detail as I got closer. Max's roadster was parked the same as I had last seen it. Awesus had returned and parked next to that. The other car I recognized, but had to convince myself it was Sal's Imperial parked on the lawn only a few feet away from Wallace's crumpled body.

I stopped when I was about ten feet from the driver's door and squinted. There was someone behind the wheel, but they either hadn't seen me or didn't mind me staring. It wasn't until I had practically leaned my arms on the door frame that I could make out the face through the open window.

"Hey there, Mr. Hamilton."

"Oh. Hello, boy."

Hamilton looked even worse than I had last seen him, holding another in a series of pistols that everyone seemed to have tucked in some offhand place. Hamilton's focus was entirely on the gun in his hands, slack in his lap. A dewy aura rose up from the weapon, the only thing seeming to attract any light in this shaded world of Max's front yard.

"Where'd you get Sal's car?"

"It was in the woods."

"What were you doing in the woods?" I noticed the dirt on his shirtfront, under his nails.

"Is Max at home?"

"I think so, yeah. I'm going to see him. Are you coming in?" He reached out for the door handle but didn't open it. "Is his man in there?"

"Awesus is in there, yeah."

"Anybody else around?"

"Wallace here. I don't think he counts, though."

Hamilton craned his head over the dash to get a better look at Wallace's stiff corpse.

"Who was he?"

"Not the feds."

"The others then? Max's people?"

"I don't think they'd say that. More like Richie's people."

"Richie…"

Hamilton reached in his jacket and handed me a small case.

I looked inside. "Samantha's diamonds?"

"She told you they were hers?" He looked confused.

"That you gave them to her."

Hamilton drew in a deep breath and moaned like he'd been stabbed. He pressed his thumb and forefinger to the bridge of his nose, talking without looking up.

"Where is she now?"

"Her mother's." I took out the wrinkled note and tossed it in his lap. He stared down at it, not opening it.

"What about Betsie?"

"Gonna head down there too. She's waiting at the diner for a lift."

"The feds will go there."

"Don't think so."

"But she… Sal."

"The feds don't seem to care much about how it happened to him. I told them I was the one who did it anyway."

"Shot him?"

"Hit him."

"With a gun?"

"Tree branch. An extraction team's coming to take care of it."

"They know where he's buried… where he is?"

"Yeah. This car's supposed to be there. Plus, all his identifying credentials. Did you see any of that stuff around?"

"It's all back there… with him." He was quiet after that.

I took out my smokes and lit a couple up for us.

The stones rattled around in the bottom of the pack.

"What about the earrings Richie gave to Betsie?"

"I have no idea."

I took them out and handed one over.

He held the thing up and lit a match, "Fake."

"You're sure?"

"I'd know. The only real stones around are the ones in that case. They sent Richie here with them from Chicago as a sort of peace offering. Perhaps business proposition is the right phrase... more like business coercion."

"Wallace said the business with Max is over. Something about a guy, DeBeers now."

"He was correct. But don't tell Max."

"Max already knows."

"And he's..."

"Last I heard he was packing it in. He's gonna leave the diamonds you guys made and take off."

"There have never been any diamonds made! No one wants any diamonds from Max. It's all a fantasy. With prohibition over, the demand for hooch is going to explode. By the Fall, the stills will be run by someone else, and they'll be laughing at imitation diamonds from Times Square."

"He says he can make real ones."

"Like his parents."

"If there's no diamonds being made, then what about these?"

I produced the sack from inside the jacket with my good arm and held it up for him to see. He recoiled and spit out the car window on the ground.

"Where did you find this?"

"Richie had it hidden with his stuff."

"Goddamnit. The tractor's in the ditch now, boy."

"Were they yours?"

"They weren't Richie's! That idiot. Fool. Ass…"

"Wallace says you were already moving stuff for DeBeers."

"The goon, what would he know."

"What about Max?"

"What about him? It's a shock he's lived this long. Especially after that show he put on in my parlor."

"You seemed pretty supportive at the time."

"Didn't we all… you're in the plays, you understand. Think of that night as a play, staged for Max to appear in, but for which he didn't know he was preparing."

"You all cut him out. Behind his back."

"Yes."

"Sold him out to the mob?"

"He is the mob! Was the mob… close enough to count."

"And the feds?"

"They came for the booze and learned of the diamonds. Or it was the other way around… or both all along. It's all become quite…" He threw up one hand and let it come down slowly, fluttering then collapsing into his lap. He hung his head and stayed like that long enough for me to finish the smoke I had started. When it was done, I left him and headed for the house.

I wondered what would happen to the Barn if the feds arrested him and what would happen to the fields and the caretakers that lived in the house and that field hand who came around twice a year to work the crops. His work in that soil could be finished right now without him even knowing it.

If Hamilton goes away, the farm could be foreclosed on. That's what happened to the Cole family down the street back home. It was different since their father had died, but the family couldn't afford to pay all those expenses and keep the house. All the families in the neighborhood came out and held signs and even donated some money, but it wasn't enough for the bank because they foreclosed on the house and pretty soon another family moved in there. I still went to school with their kid, he's a couple of years younger than me. I used to play with the Cole kid too when he lived there—the house was the closest to the park. I never heard from him after he moved away. It's easy to forget about people, especially when they're gone.

I remembered something I meant to ask Hamilton and turned around in time to see the muzzle flash through the windshield. A dent raised from the roof of the car. A noise I was growing accustomed to. White smoke issued from the open window. I didn't care to go see what it concealed.

The hastily hung drapes were the only things that had changed since I left. The main ballroom was still a mess. Max's study, littered with glass. There seemed to be an audible hum coming from the next room, but when I moved, the source would follow so that I was always in the center of the fade. An encapsulated seed in a wall of sound. I put my hand against the doorframe. The wood responded as if alive. I pressed my ear against the varnish—a resounding orchestra of pine. There was some commotion back in the study, and I looked to see Max go into the kitchen with a stack of text-books.

He didn't hear me approach over the beehive drone.

"Hey there, Max." He spun around wearing his pajamas and dressing gown, books still in his hands. His face was waxy and pale. The sweat stood out on his chest, where the skin was exposed. He grinned wide, hair falling in front of his eyes, not bothering to push it aside.

"Joseph! And without a moment to spare."

"You taking all those when you leave?" The books I meant.

"I'm not going anywhere."

"Where's Awesus?"

"With the generators, which should be running full boat by now. Come! There's little time."

I knocked the books out of his hands, "That's what I'm trying to tell you. I got what diamonds there are. You gotta get out of here."

"What diamonds?"

"The stash! Wallace's buddies are at Hamilton's, and they'll be here soon."

"Good. They'll be witness to the next evolution of their trade. Let them take that back to Chicago with them."

"They'll kill you and take the stash. The diamonds–"

"The diamonds are fakes! Not synthetic, simply counterfeit."

"What about these?" I produced the sack from inside my coat. Max snatched it away.

"These were Richie's?"

"Hamilton's."

He shoved his hand into the bag and pulled out a grip of the stones, letting them sluice out between his fingers. "Fakes! Not even very good. Were they peddling the things to hookers and schoolboys? Where is Hamilton now?"

"I saw him outside."

"Will he be joining us anytime soon?"

"I don't think so."

He threw the rest of the stones at the wall, dropped the sack, letting it spill on the ground, "This is what those half-wits expect for quality? Wait until they see what a real diamond looks like."

"Hamilton said they sent this along too. 'A sample', he said of the real product."

His face changed when he saw the case. It was an average earring box: black velvet, no markings. But there was something about it he recognized. Something drew his hand out toward it. I thought he would grab it, but he reached past, grasping onto my arm where I was shot. The pain of it was quickly overcome by the urge to puke. He released and flexed, and I could feel the gash open up under the bandage. I swallowed a mouthful of panicky saliva, breathed through my nose. The warm red stuff ran down my wrist.

*still burning.*

I woke up on the ground with my face in the pile of counterfeits. Max was hunched down over me, caressing the top of my head. I was having a hard time making things out through what I thought was smoke, but was probably the early stages of a concussion messing with my vision. He held the now open jewel case in his free hand, rubbing his thumb across the rocks.

"These belonged to your mother. To my mother before that. The only thing of hers which survived the fire. The flame he cannot shut out. I'm glad to have them back... though I don't much care for their connotation."

The house took up a higher whining pitch, and Max looked all around us as if he could see the reverb. I lifted my head, brushing off the diamonds where they had stuck to my cheek. Streaks of blood on my palm. Max helped me up and propped me against the counter. He grabbed the books, handed me a few.

"Come now, son. We have work to do."

Max lead me down the rabbit hole hallway, dropping books like bread crumbs. I stumbled along, not keeping up.

The open cellar door rattled on its hinges. The generator stood, half-obscured behind an elephant door opposite the line of stills. A few cables, thick as my arm lead from the generator to a pyramid of concrete bricks where they connected to some pieces of metal on either side. Max dumped the books on the ground with some others next to a workbench and began tinkering with something he found there. The cellar door opened in the far wall, and Awesus jumped down from outside. He went to the closest pallet and started hauling wooden cases of booze onto the loading platform. I tossed the books aside and went over to him. He didn't stop to acknowledge me, kept moving the crates and stacking them up.

"Max has gone nuts. You gotta get him out of here."

Awesus paused to watch Max work—spilling powder: white and red and silver into a cauldron, getting the stuff on the workbench, his face, cursing himself—then resumed his stacking.

"Wallace was telling the truth. He's got buddies on the way, probably the feds after that. What are you gonna do?"

What he did was crank up the platform and start unloading his stack out through the cellar doors. He had been loading the cases onto the pontoon boat and already had a pretty good haul set aside.

"Where will you go?"

"Far," he said and lowered the platform again, closing the door behind us before starting in on the next pallet.

Across the room, Max placed his elemental concoction into the yellowy bricks. Space was allowed at either end for two metal prongs to be inserted, and the whole thing went on the top of his foundry. He appeared to be satisfied, and activated a breaker that connected the wiring. Electricity jolted through the metal prongs from either side of the yellow brick which reddened with heat but didn't crack.

The generator mellowed, soothed from the release of energy, and stayed at a constant but much quieter hum. It was soft enough to hear the stamping feet clodding through the upstairs rooms.

Awesus heard, and paused his stacking.

Max heard nothing but the sparking electricity of creation. The steps were in the hallway now. Awesus drew out the gun he was always packing: a hulking wood gripped automatic.

The door to the hall opened slowly. The generator cranked up, the drone intensified. The light from the Frankenstein barbecue pit threw jagged shadows across the floor. Max shielded his eyes, trying not to look away. Big guy and Skinny walked in, followed by two other look-alike tough guys. They stood inside the basement entrance, looking all around at what was no doubt an impressive setup. Awesus took that time to level the automatic and pop off a few rounds, catching Tough Guy Number One in the shoulder and sending him to the ground. The others scattered, taking cover behind the many pallets of booze, and returned fire. Max's daze was broken by the intrusion. Bullets tore open the wooden cases and ripped into the polished stills drawing out the high octane makings of the best prohibition whiskey this side of Appalachia.

I crouched behind a steel drum which dinged sickeningly each time a hunk of lead bounced off. I found Betsie's, one round left revolver in my jacket and stuck the muzzle around the drum, fired it blindly before flinging the damn thing aside.

Awesus stood tall nearby, firing rhythmically at our attackers. He reached his free hand to his waistband and produced another automatic, which I thought he would toss to me but instead held aloft, moving closer to his targets with every shot, not letting them escape their failing cover.

Max took a knee, drawing a revolver from his ankle and fired carefully, picking off Tough Guy Number Two.

The generator surged, throwing the ceiling lights out of whack. The metal conductors shot sparks into the brick oven, casting more crazy firework shadows.

Awesus hunkered down a few pallets ahead of me, shoving cartridges into empty chambers. Bottles of booze exploded all around him, light brown splatters on his perfect suit. Big Guy and Skinny moved together, getting closer, only a few stacks away from Awesus.

Max had resumed his station at the brick oven tracing his hand along wires frantically. Running to the generator, ignoring barely missed killing shots. Adjustments were made to the current.

Awesus reloaded.

Big Guy and Skinny advanced.

Awesus ducked out to the side and around, putting himself parallel to the goons, a sight trained on each.

Max's scream cut through the air before I saw the flames roaring overhead, coating the ceiling in fire.

The generator squealed before smoke poured out the vents, followed by more licking hot flame eating up the ethanol bleeding from the stills.

The eruption knocked us all back on our asses. Hunks of metal and rock were flung into the air. Big Guy took half a brick in the side of his face, crushing his skull like a deflated basketball. Skinny landed and rolled, coating himself in one hundred proof, soaking up the fire, burning to a crisp. Tough Guy Number One limped toward the door to the hallway and would have made it if a nearby still hadn't gone off like a bomb, throwing him into the air, snapping his neck against the closest wall. Another still exploded, and the fire spread to the next. I dragged my way over to Awesus, lazily slouched against the remnants of a pallet.

The fire had completely surrounded us. I could see the top layer of my skin reddening, hair starting to singe. I found a bottle of the good stuff and gulped about half of it down. I held it out for Awesus, but he didn't take it. His eyes landed on his hands, his legs, and he shook his head. I held the bottle up to his lips and let him have a mouthful, not knowing if he could swallow. Another still went off, pushing the fire closer to us. I finished what I could of the bottle but was having a hard time breathing. I thought I might pass out before I had a chance to burn to death, which was comforting. The ceiling started to crumble away.

"Hey, Awes?"

He looked over at me.

"You didn't kill Richie, did you?"

His face set in a frown, blood in the corners of his mouth.

He didn't move again after that. I couldn't keep my eyes open any longer and didn't really need to. I could see everything as I rose up out of my body and above flames. The stills kept exploding, but I couldn't hear them. The fire was all around, but I couldn't feel it. The smoke was getting thicker, but my vision was clear.

Max stumbled out from a heap of burning rubble, skin bubbling, hair and scalp missing, clothes and shoes on fire. I thought I saw something glimmer in his melting hand, a memory. Then the fire swept through, and there was nothing left. I could see through the ceiling and was lifted, relieved by the sudden cool darkness of the unknown.

*summer's almost gone.*

My afterlife was interrupted by the clanging pulley of the loading platform. Vicky yanked on the steel chain, hand over hand, ignoring the fire sneaking out the cellar door. She rolled me into the sand to stop my clothes from burning and helped me up on my feet.

"Hey there, Vicky."

"Hey there, yourself."

I leaned on her until we were on the level surface of Max's backyard. Smoke rose out of craters where the earth had fallen in. The fire crept over the grass surrounding the mound that hid the cellar door, groped at the dry trees along the river setting the leaves ablaze.

She left me there swaying on the lawn, returning from the river-bank backward, dragging a case of the good stuff. I managed a hand hold, and we walked the long way around Max's with the crate hanging between us.

Fire had spread upstairs and was eating away at the curtains on the first floor, revealing empty rooms like innards.

Tables and chairs burning white and green and red, books falling from shelves turned to ash, the ceilings layered in soot as the flames moved to consume the second story.

The driveway was longer and darker than ever on the walk back. I realized my ears were ringing and that Vicky had been talking for I don't know how long. I watched her gesture with her free hand, eyes wide in telling some vital detail, grip tight on our payload, carrying most of the weight, "…she had called their mother from the road and came back to get her. They were gone an hour after you. It was Lloyd's idea to come back down here, something about you being a friend of the family."

Lloyd was standing outside the parked hack. He helped us get the case into the back seat and then helped me in next to it. We heard the sirens and were already a good way down the road by the time any lights were flashing. Lloyd drove us undirected, letting the outside whip through the open windows. I took out my smokes, forgetting I had given my last to Hamilton. All I had left was Betsie's earrings clattering around together down in the bottom of the pack. I crumpled them up in the package and tossed it. I tapped Lloyd on the shoulder and held up two fingers. He threw me a fresh pack, and I lit up for us all.

We wound up at the pier in Old Orchard Beach. It was getting pretty late, and people out dancing and on dates eating ice cream at the pier were milling around, hoping not to call it a night too soon and thinking of the best ways to get back to where they were going or preferably someplace better.

We cracked into the case with a tire iron and worked on a bottle of the good stuff together, watching everyone come and go.

*

I was arrested alone the next day, trying to get my things from the Barn. Captain Montgomery asked me a lot of questions about Max and Hamilton and the house in Elliot and even mentioned the FBI. He didn't ask a lot about why I knew what I did, and when I asked if I was going to have to talk to the feds, he called my father and asked him to please come pick me up.

The next couple of months were spent growing back my hair and learning how to move my fingers again. I had to start school late and ended up having to take summer classes, so I didn't go back to the Barn the next year. I got in touch with Vicky a couple times, mostly late at night after all her dishes were done, and the grill had been scraped cleaned. She never heard from Samantha or Betsie and found out their father's house had been sold. A different family owns the Barn now but they still do the plays there.

The hay in the fields has grown tall and soon a group of field hands will return to cut and bale the offshoots from the soil which has been sown and reaped since before they were born, probably will be long after they're buried in it.

www.ingramcontent.com/pod-product-compliance
Lightning Source LLC
Chambersburg PA
CBHW070627130626
46555CB00006B/2467